Return to Leiper's Fork

A Leiper's Fork Love Story

Penny Garrison

Return to Leiper's Fork

Copyright©2012 by Penny Garrison

No part of this book shall be reproduced or transmitted in any form or by any means, electronic or mechanical including photocopying, recording or by any information storage and retrieval system without permission in writing from the copyright owner.

This is a work of fiction. Names, characters and incidents either are the product of the author's imagination or are used fictitiously and any resemblance to any actual persons living or dead, with exception to noted figures in the Leiper's Fork community and Colonel Jesse Steed and other historical figures are entirely coincidental.

This book was printed in the United States of America

Copyright © 2012 Penny Garrison

ISBN-13-978-1478381495
ISBN-10-1478381493

All rights reserved.

Dedication

This book is dedicated to the historic community of Leiper's Fork, Tennessee and to the efforts of leaders, especially Aubrey Preston, Bruce and Marty Hunt and other visionaries, who believe in Leiper's Fork and invest deeply into it. Leiper's Fork is one of the most unique towns in our country.

I have enjoyed each visit and your annual Christmas Parade is what inspired me to write this book. It is definitely the most interesting parade in the world and I will never forget it. Little did I know there was an effort to preserve your quaint, beautiful and historic village until I finished my manuscript and came across a few pages concerning the encroaching suburban development. It was then, I made a few changes. God bless each one of you for believing in your community and seeing it blossom so beautifully. Keep those Christmas lights burning and keep fiddling and dancing at the Lawn Chair Theater.

This book is also dedicated to Grant and Nicole in honor of their October wedding. Jim and I will finally have a daughter who was a real Pork Industry Princess. Thinking of you two inspired me to write many things, but especially the one hundred gold coins, the wedding dress with touches of blue, the square cut diamond and most of all your wedding at Boone Hall Plantation, Charleston, South Carolina. Even though you're not allowed to etch your initials in glass at the lovely plantation home, I hope you dance beneath the Avenue of Oaks.

Acknowledgements

To April Cantrell, at Leiper's Fork Visitor's Center, thanks for responding when I needed help. You certainly stand in the gap for Leiper's Fork. You were a blessing, as was Leiper's Fork Foundation and Deborah Warnick, who allowed me to use her photo for the front cover. It spoke volumes.

Return to Leiper's Fork

Table of Contents

Dedication
Acknowledgements
Leiper's Fork

1. The Painting
2. Looking Back
3. The Crisis
4. The Confession
5. The Meeting
6. The Romance
7. The Reunion
8. The Decision 46
9. Engaged
10. The Exhibit
11. Dinner for Two
12. The Visitor
13. Yard Sales
14. The Conversation
15. Thanksgiving
16. Gold Coins
17. Christmas Parade
18. The Dedication
19. The Confrontation
20. Memories
21. The Promise
22. The Dance

Leiper's Fork Poem

Leiper's Fork

Long before settlers arrived on the rich fertile soil, known today as Leiper's Fork, Tennessee, prehistoric Indians roamed the land and claimed it as their communal hunting grounds. Later, these same Indians became known as the Cherokee, Chickasaw and Shawnee. Their endless supply of relics found in pastures and along creek beds date back 4,000 years.

Numerous settlers arrived from Virginia and North Carolina during the late 1790's to claim land promised them, as payment for their services during the Revolutionary War. One of those settlers was none other than the war hero, Colonel Jesse Steed, who settled on part of the 2,504 acre land grant that was later sold to Jesse Benton, father of Thomas Hart Benton, a future United States senator from Missouri.

Through the years, the Adams, Parham, Wilkin, Locke, Benton, Cummins and Bond families, along with numerous others, joined the brave folk whose desire was to create a beautiful community. They decided to settle along one road, Old Hillsboro, in the shadow of Franklin, ten miles away.

They named their town Leiper's Fork, after the Leiper family which settled much of the land along the creek that passed through the village. Later, the Middle Tennessee Railroad was built and as a result, a bank, lumber mills, blacksmith shops, churches, a school, a college and a poor farm sprang up in the town.

Today, Leiper's Fork is the only rural historic village on the Tennessee portion of the Natchez Trace Parkway. It is there, off the beaten path where the rugged and weathered peaks meet the clouds, that this love story had its beginning.

Return to Leiper's Fork

Chapter 1: The Painting

"Jesse Steed! Why, dear God did you allow him to come here today?"

Rachel Benton, a widow of only a few days, whispered softly, and looked down at the fresh dark sod at her feet. Had Jesse come to Leiper's Fork after a decade, to pay his respects to the widow of a classmate or begin developing the land he had inherited on his parent's death? Gossip was he had come to town to purchase more land and develop the hundreds of acres which fringed Leiper's Fork, a tiny historic community ten miles south of Franklin. Rachel's beloved town was threatened with progress, if suburban development was considered progress. Now, the scenic farmlands were threatened and Leiper's Fork, its land and way of life would one day be destroyed.

Now, a soft summer rain gently fell and dripped down the multi-paned window of the rustic oak cabin, a short distance from Leiper's Fork. Rachel Benton quietly laid down her brush and turned from the large canvass. She tried to forget days like this. The drizzling rain reminded her of the sweet scent of flowers and her eyes brimmed with fresh tears.

Flowers!

Rachel breathed in the fresh air and thought how the day reminded her of her husband's funeral, one year ago.

How often Randall had told her, if he could, he would pick every flower in Leiper's Fork, wrap them in ribbons and lay them at her feet. The day of his funeral, rain fell softly and numerous bouquets of flowers were at her feet but they were not from Randall. Friends, family and students sent them to show their love for Leiper's Fork, popular, young basketball coach. Known simply as, "Coach," Randall Benton had valiantly fought the enemy that ravaged his strong body but the enemy had gained the victory. Randall's basketball team had worshipped its hardworking coach but it was left in the hands of a grieving assistant, Stu Trimble. Rachel was left in the arms of her parents and her God.

The day of Randall's burial, Rachel lifted her large, brown eyes to watch the gray clouds slowly drift across the sky and seemingly touch the craggy peaks. The clouds reminded her of the set of steel-gray eyes of a man she had known _ a man she had loved long ago.

The tall man had stared at her that day through the crowd of mourners and as his gaze locked with hers, she lifted her hand in surprise and noticed a flicker of emotion cloud his handsome face. He mouthed her name then raked his hand through his thick, dark glossy hair. As he blinked, she remembered his long dark lashes and how they set off his beautiful serene eyes. With a backward glance, the well-dressed man turned to be swallowed in a sea of mourners.

Jesse Steed!

Jesse had left for college immediately after their breakup and eventually married the cool reserved Susanna Southall, who considered herself a step above most seniors in her graduating class. He had graduated with a degree in business, and later inherited Steedmore, Leiper's Fork historical mansion. Now, before the town could catch its breath, Leiper's Fork would be a stage and Jesse Steed would be marching down Old Hillsboro Road located a stone's throw from the famous Natchez Parkway.

All of Leiper's Fork would take notice and one day, tell their grandchildren and great grandchildren, how different the town had been before Jesse Steed and his army of engineers arrived. They'd tell about large trees that had stood for centuries and long, gray stone walls built by settlers. They would speak of the beautiful rolling, green hills, once dotted with buttery rolls of yellow hay and rich fields of black soil, which had been tilled and planted and prayed over by farmers. John Deere tractors would no longer lumber across the fields which at one time had been home to deer and wild turkey. The creeks that had once drained the fields would be diverted and no longer would the rains run down the roofs, rush into ravines and plunge into the creek below. Their comforting gurgling sounds in summer would be lost to men forever and the few animals that dared to search for water would be unable to slip to the creek's edge for a cool drink. In Leiper's Fork, almost everyone would bow down to Jesse Steed except the wise ones who remembered the land in bygone days and one of them would include a young woman who had sworn to protect her charming

Return to Leiper's Fork

village.

"He'd sell his own soul to the devil. That's exactly what he'd do!" Rachel cried out in frustration but the rain seemed not to hear. Instead, it dripped slowly down the shake roof, forming puddles, which later filled ravines and rushed wildly to tumble through underbrush, into the creeks surrounding the quaint historic village.

With a swipe of her paintbrush, she angrily smeared gray oils at the top of the canvass. "If I have to, I will face him alone!" Furiously, she mixed in other colors and swore to herself, she would face Jesse Steed, who would immediately back off and leave town when he saw how angry she could be.

"I'll take him to court, if I have to. I'll get a court order and he'll leave us alone. He's just another big city guy, coming back to destroy us and all we stand for. He's probably ashamed he grew up here." Rachel painted long into the night and in the wee hours of morning stood back to appraise her work. "An angry sky! That's exactly how I feel. Angry! But just like Scarlett O'Hare, I will fight and if I have to eat radishes the rest of my life, I will save Leiper's Fork from Jesse and his army of engineers and developers. Just wait until he sees all of us fight him in court. He'll turn tail and run back to San Francisco, as fast as he can. He'll wish he'd never set his expensive Italian loafers on Williamson County soil." At that moment, a voice within her whispered what she'd always known, but refused to believe.

You always loved Jesse Steed. You tried to bury your feelings but it is time to face the truth. One day, you will come face to face, with your heart.

Later, warm sunshine invaded the wooded hills of Leiper's Fork and trails of vapor curled lazily from the forest floor and floated above the weathered hills to join the white cumulus above. At first glance, outsiders thought the vapor was smoke but the tiny Tennessee community knew it was an everyday occurrence which made their hills that much more enduring.

Rachel worked on, too exhausted to notice. After stopping to breakfast on toast, slathered with homemade peach preserves, she sipped her coffee in the stillness that dominated the cabin. Again, she painted into the night, avoiding the phone whose shrill cry disturbed her but only momentarily.

After the hills and vales were covered once again, in the cloak of darkness, Rachel stood back almost too exhausted to view her work. As she peered closer, she was stunned. The tiny village she had created was Leiper's Fork. A long brown road led through the town and in the distance, rolling hills sprinkled with round bales of buttery hay dotted the landscape. The angry, gray sky threatened rain but in the midst of the gray heavens, a thread of golden sunshine pierced the sky and spread its rays over the small clapboard church. Rachel's hands flew to her face as she gasped in astonishment.

"This painting represents my promise to Randall! There is hope when things seem dark. Leiper's Fork will be saved from Jesse's grasp or I'll die trying." In tiny letters, the young widow carefully entitled the painting. The Promise- Rachel Benton

Fresh tears surfaced, as she remembered the vow she had made to the husband, over a year ago. Randall had only smiled weakly. She remembered his response, that early June morning, as the sun streamed through the beautiful log home which sat on two acres, a short distance from downtown, Leiper's Fork.

"I can't let Jesse Steed ruin our town and all it has stood for, so he can feather his pockets with millions of dollars. Randall, I will never allow anyone to destroy us. I'll fight tooth and toenail to keep Leiper's Fork the historic village it has always been. Your ancestors and mine settled and built this town. Let Nashville drown in concrete. This town means the world to me and I won't give up until all of the fight is gone out of me. No matter what it costs, I'll do everything I can, even if I'm broken in the process."

Randall had smiled weakly. "I know you will protect Leiper's Fork my darling and I'll keep watch. When you see heaven smiling, you'll know I'm happy about what you've done. Remember, you are only one person and Jesse is a very wealthy and influential man. But remember, when you see the sunshine you can be happy because I too, will be happy. You'll know joy once again after I'm gone. Remember the sunshine."

Rachel's face blurred, as Randall, seized with pain, gasped for air. At the same time panic filled him and he fell back against his pillows.

Return to Leiper's Fork

Jesse has always loved Rachel. Will he return for her after I'm gone

Chapter 2: Looking Back

A year had passed since Randall's funeral and the large painting she'd started months after his death hung above the massive fieldstone fireplace, he had built. Each time Rachel glanced at it, her resolve to save Leiper's Fork was strengthened. But talk of Jesse Steed and his new development had died after the funeral. Rarely was his name mentioned and people said, he'd moved on to greener pastures _ it had all been talk.

Gossip had blossomed quickly about Rachel and how she had shunned Jesse at the funeral dinner that day. People said he left quickly looking hurt _ he'd only tried to console the grieving widow. When he reached out to touch her, she had jerked her arm, as if his touch burned her skin.

"Don't! Please!"

After needing to sort through her emotions, Rachel had escaped to the coolness of the women's restroom refusing to leave. Grandmotherly Mrs. Turner, gently patted Jesse's shoulder and murmured, "Now, now, Jesse. She's just overcome with grief. I've known Rachel all her life and she didn't mean a thing by it." He'd turned to Mrs. Locke, Rachel's mother who was horrified Rachel had been so cruel. After all, Jesse was only paying his respects to Randall's widow. Jesse whispered to Mrs. Locke, "Please tell Rachel I meant no harm. I just want her to know I care. I'll send a card."

He left in his late model Mercedes and the delivery of a beautiful bouquet of pink and red roses the next day were promptly pitched in Rachel's trash. The note accompanying them went unread. Rachel cried. "I want nothing from you, Jesse. You don't have the love in your whole body, my Randall had in his little finger. I hope I never see you again, unless it's in court and I can't wait to see the look on your face when you run away like a coon dog after it's been sprayed by a skunk. You'll have your tail tucked between your legs like ole Willie. Don't ever think of coming to town, to destroy my Leiper's Fork."

Rachel laughed, after remembering the last year. Jesse had evidently forgotten to return. She kicked up her heels and danced all the way to her

Return to Leiper's Fork

bathroom. She had a date with her bubble bath. As she turned the faucets, her arms, neck and back ached but she was ready to wash away the scent of paints and every ache and pain in her body. As she relaxed in the slipper tub, she smiled. Randall had told her when they built the cabin some years before his sickness, he couldn't get her a glass slipper but he could put in a slipper tub. Now, she leaned back against the smooth China fixture and closed her eyes. What had happened in her life? She found herself mumbling, as she pushed back a long strand of golden brown hair, then closed her eyes and sank deeper in the warm water.

"I remember walking down Old Hillsboro Road, when I was in high school and watching a green truck make its way through town. It seems like yesterday and it has been years. Out of nowhere, I heard a voice."

"Hey! Want a ride?" Randall Benton looked out at her, after wiping the seat and throwing his gym clothes under it. A huge smile lit his face, causing his large, brown eyes to sparkle. As she stared at the basketball star wondering what to say, he opened the truck door. "No sense walking, when I can take you anywhere you want to go." He motioned her into the truck, as a car passed on his left. "Where to, Your Royal Highness? This Ford may be a ninety-two but she's faithful and true just like the woman I'm going to marry one day, after I graduate from college. Got to get that education before I'm dragged to the altar. However, my angel will be a whole lot prettier and classier than my Betsy, here." He patted the dashboard gently.

"Sorry, ole girl, but I really mean it. You are old, but you're faithful." He smiled and turned toward Rachel. "Got to be good to my girl, you know. Can't get to work and school without her, even if she carries a few dents." He laughed nervously, very aware that a beautiful, young senior had agreed to ride in his dilapidated truck. Randall drove slowly down the two lane road, known as Old Hillsboro Road. Every minute with Rachel Locke was golden.

"Randall Benton, I thought that looked like you but beneath that ragged ball cap I wasn't sure." Rachel laughed in relief.

The tall, dark haired Randall smiled radiantly. "Now that you've hurt my feelings and made fun of my favorite cap, you'd better apologize to Mr. Cap. Tell me where you're going and I'll drop you off."

Rachel laughed. "Randall, I didn't have a specific plan to go anywhere. I was walking to clear my head. Right now, I'm not too sure if I'm of sound mind or not." Rachel's eyes burned but she blinked away the tears.

Randall studied her intently. "Wouldn't have anything to do with the talk at school, about you and Jesse would it?" At the mention of Jesse's name, Rachel nodded and tears streamed down her face. Randall touched her arm. "Hey now! I didn't cause those did I? If I did, please forgive me. It is none of my business. Okay?" He pulled a Kleenex from his pocket.

"Benton doesn't allow tears in his car, unless they're about him. They might wash out some of the dust. Come on, princess. Let's drive down to the Lawn Chair Theater and talk. If it's not too late for you, we can have soda and pizza at Puckett's or a sandwich and chips at The Country Store. You can cry on Dr. Randall's shoulder anytime and he'll work his magic. After spending time with him, you'll never cry again, unless it's for joy. That's a promise, Miss Locke. Are you ready for me to spin my magic?"

Rachel tried to laugh as he parked his dusty truck, and slowly leaned over to cup her chin.

"Now, don't open your door until I get to the other side. A gentleman doesn't let his Royal Highness, open her carriage door. It will only take me a second, so sit tight." Afterward, he led her to a picnic table where he wiped the bench with one hand and sat down beside her. "You know, I melt when women cry and we don't want that to happen, do we, Miss Locke? If it does, you'll have to drive yourself home."

"Hopefully, that won't happen but thanks, Randall. I feel better already." Rachel smiled, as he caressed her chin with his large hand.

"You know, to be an artist you're kind of cute." He sniffed the air and smiled. "Don't even smell like turpentine."

"Randall Benton. I have not painted all week. Of course I don't smell like turpentine."

He laughed and searched her face. His eyes grew large and he tried to smile, but blushed. So did Rachel. The tall, good looking student who had recently been voted, Most Athletic, by the senior class was studying her lips.

Return to Leiper's Fork

The student voted, Tennessee's Most Artistic, moistened them and looked away. Randall Benton was not only a star on the basketball court, but a star academically. Talk was, he had been offered several scholarships to top universities but Randall knew he wanted to go to the closest one possible. So did Rachel. As he inched closer, she became embarrassed and looked away. She knew that look and Randall wanted more than friendship. As he placed his hand on her shoulder, Randall exhaled. He remembered Rachel Locke belonged to Jesse Steed, a wealthy senior with a very bright future.

He held her hand. "I've got to choose a college close to home so I can look in on my parents, from time to time. Dad's not strong like he was and Mom's worn out from taking care of him. If the jack had not slipped when he was working on the car, life would be different but God knows all about that."

Rachel looked at him, surprised that he talked so easily about God when many seniors were embarrassed or ashamed to mention His name. He stared back in surprise.

"What?" He smiled warmly, as his large eyes searched hers.

"You mentioned God as if He were your best friend. I like that."

"Well, I hope I don't offend you or send you running but God is my best friend. Matter of fact, we talk a lot and He's cool." Randall chuckled. "I've seen you enter those church doors Miss Locke. I think you know how cool, God is."

"Well, yes. I don't say a lot but I'd never turn my back on God. Without Him, I'd be a mess." It was that very conversation that changed how Rachel Locke viewed Randall Benton. No longer was he the lanky, handsome basketball player who drove an old green truck and wore a ragged John Deere ball cap. After today, he was more. He understood her and Rachel liked that. A picture of Jesse flashed in her mind. As far as she knew, Jesse had never darkened the door of a church.

"Miss Locke, if you need to talk to Dr. Randall, just call and make an appointment and he'll see you, as soon as possible. His appointment book stays closed now days, since he needs more time to study for finals and work at the hardware store but he always makes time for very special patients." He grinned and Rachel noticed how beautiful his smile was. His lips were full and firm and he had dimples in his cheeks. Randall had a reputation for working hard and playing hard and she loved his long, lean athletic build and tanned skin. His cheeks were rosy and she knew he was the type of man who would always look younger than he actually was. With his big hands and broad muscular shoulders, he could pick her up and twirl her around before she knew it. When he'd reached across to open her door, his freshly shaven face had touched hers and his scent reminded her of the smell of clean air after a soft summer rain.

Randall was known not only as an unusual athlete but as the only athlete who never dated. Some said he had little money and some said it was because no high school female would be seen riding in his old truck. It was true that money in the Benton household was scarce. It was also true that it bothered Randall if a date had to ride in his Ford-100, regardless of how he cleaned it. His job at the hardware store left little money, after he gave most of his check to his mother. Dating could be expensive and times were tough at his house. Mrs. Benton cleaned houses and took in ironings to make ends meet. A scholarship was the only way to college and Randall knew if he wanted to get somewhere in life, he would have to get an education. Pizza had cost him but it had been his chance to spend time with the popular senior, Rachel Locke. He would have to work extra hours the next week to make up for it.

"In the future, princess, watch those tears. You don't want Jesse Steed to think you're spending time with, Mr. Kleenex. There are greater things to do than cry over a lost cause, if you know what I mean. You never know when a knight in shining armor might ride up on a horse and sweep you off your tiny little feet." His face turned serious. "Now, knights don't appreciate crying women. Tears can rust their armor, you know. So get out of Ole Betsy and cheer up, angel. I've got to get home and study."

Rachel laughed, as he playfully opened her door and shooed her up the walk. She enjoyed spending time with the guy she had only seen on the basketball court and in the halls. She had dated Jesse since December but she liked the way Randall listened when she talked. Rachel also liked his humor and the fact that he seemed to be humble and grateful for what he had. Their conversation had gone deeper than she had planned and as she got ready for bed that night, Rachel remembered her question.

Return to Leiper's Fork

"Dr. Randall, what do I owe for this session?"

Looking very serious, Randall had spoken. "Well, Miss Benton, I'll send a bill as usual. My office manager will have to prepare it and it usually takes a day." The next day, Randall stood waiting at the door of her English class. As Rachel came rushing out, he pulled her aside. "Special delivery, Miss Locke." Turning quickly, Rachel watched as Randall handed her an envelope and without a backward glance strolled down the hall toward the gym. Astonished, she slipped the card from the envelope. As she read the scrawled note, her face turned as red as a leaf on a maple tree in fall.

One kiss due tomorrow. Dr. Randall Benton

"The nerve of that guy! How can he expect me, to do that? I hardly know him, but he is nice." Smiling, Rachel walked away, wondering what it would be like to kiss the tall dark haired basketball player with the quick smile and large sparkling eyes. He wasn't as wealthy as Jesse and he didn't live in a mansion but she'd ride in Ole Betsy, again, dust or no dust.

On Friday, true to fashion, Randall stood outside her last class. Surprised for the second time in two days, Rachel asked, "How do you know my class schedule, Dr. Benton?"

"It appears, Dr. Benton has friends in high places, Miss Locke. Drop a compliment or two, on Miss Beasley and she'll tell you anything you want to know. Spinsters do that, if you treat them right. Seriously, I know your schedule frontwards and backwards. Our school isn't that big. Besides, I've only watched you from a distance for most of my life. May I walk you to your car and collect for my bill?" Randall rubbed the side of his face in embarrassment as Rachel watched him blush. How bold he was and yet how shy. Randall Benton was a guy she wanted to spend more time with.

"Randall, you silly. You can walk me to my car if you carry my bag. However, I had to park in the last spot which must be at least a mile from the building." She giggled, after seeing the surprised look on his face. "Well, maybe not a mile but it sure seemed like one this morning. As far as paying my bill, I'll have to give you fudge. Does the thought of fresh, homemade peanut butter fudge make your mouth water, Doc?" Randall laughed, reached for her heavy school bag and casually tossed it over his shoulder.

As they neared the blue Chevy, Randall reached for her key. Swiftly he unlocked the door and pitched her bag in the back seat. "It's time I collect for my services, Miss Locke." He pulled her near and after looking in her eyes, quickly kissed her cheek. Rachel's mouth sprang open in surprise, especially when she thought he would kiss her lips. Stepping back, Randall bumped into something. "What, the . . ." He turned to see a very angry Jesse.

"Rachel! What is this bumpkin doing here? Is he forcing his affection on you?" Not waiting for her answer, Jesse turned angrily, to an amused Randall. "Listen, Benton. Beat it!"

Rachel stepped between the two students. "Jesse! Mind your own business. I'm old enough to take care of myself and no, he was not forcing himself on me. I was the one who said he could kiss me."

"You said he could, what? And what did he mean about collecting for his services?" Turning, he pointed his index finger at Randall. "Listen, Basketball Boy! If I ever catch you trying to collect anything from Rachel, you'll pay big time before the sun sets. Remember that."

"Now don't get out of sorts, Jesse. Nothing has happened between us, so far. It's not your decision anyway. It's Rachel's." Randall stood back as Rachel turned to Jesse.

"Jesse! That is enough! Randall has been the perfect gentleman and we had an inside joke. That's all."

"I don't appreciate another guy kissing you, Rachel." Jesse stepped closer, lowered his voice to a whisper and held her shoulders. "I need to talk to you about next week. You've refused to take my calls." A blush crept up Jesse's handsome face as he brushed back his dark hair and looked first at Randall then at Rachel. "I need to know the color of your gown for prom, so I can order your corsage."

Rachel's voice softened, as she stared into his soft gray eyes mixed with embarrassment and anger. "Jesse, you're just a bit late and a bit forgetful. I thought we broke up two weeks ago. I don't remember us getting back together." She looked at Randall who appeared embarrassed. This conversation didn't involve him, yet he was concerned for Rachel. Rachel

Return to Leiper's Fork

hoped and prayed he would understand what was going on. "Jesse, Randall has asked me to prom and I accepted. It's too late for you and me. Too late, forever and I mean it."

As she placed her key in the ignition, Rachel smiled and gazed into Randall's wide eyes. "Randall, you asked about my gown. It's a lavender strapless. I think you'll love it. I spent a lot of time looking for it, in Nashville." With those words, she quietly drove away, leaving two astonished men standing in the parking lot. The one with dark sparkling eyes stood in disbelief, while the other stalked to his red convertible.

That night, Mrs. Locke, called Rachel to the phone. "Honey, a very nice young man wants to speak to you."

Please Lord! Don't let it be Jesse.

"H . . . Hello!" Rachel gripped the phone, wondering what she would say if it were Jesse.

"Rachel, this is Randall. Were you serious today or buffaloing Jesse?"

"About what, Randall?"

"You know what I'm talking about, Rachel."

"Oh, that. I didn't want Jesse to know I was going to prom alone. I had to do some fast thinking. I'm sorry I had to involve you but I knew if I didn't, he wouldn't take no, for an answer. I only hope I didn't cause problems for you."

Randall cleared his throat. "Rachel, I haven't asked anyone to prom. I thought about it but I thought I might have to work. To be honest, I didn't have any reason to go. Mom said, if I miss my prom, I'd regret it. Moms are usually right you know."

"Randall, let's don't disappoint your mother. How about picking me up in your carriage, at six o'clock? Only the green one will do. I kind of like Ole Betsy. Miss Locke will be patiently waiting in her lavender gown and don't order a corsage. I want to make one out of Mom's pink tea roses.

They're at bud stage now so in a few days they'll be lovely. Good night and thanks, Dr. Randall."

Randall gulped, "Sure Rachel." Randall knew a trim was in order for his dark curly locks and his black Sunday suit would have to be pressed. Later, after he'd studied for finals at the kitchen table, the athlete with the promising career whistled softly. He was taking the popular Rachel Locke to the senior prom. God was a God of miracles but Randall knew God didn't clean up dirty trucks.

Being roused by her phone, Rachel sat up in the tub.

Did I go to sleep?

How long she'd slept, she wasn't sure but the bath water was already cool. "My goodness! I was more relaxed than I thought." Wrapping a pink towel around her, she hurried to the phone but the caller hung up, as she grabbed her cell.

"Jesse Steed! It's been a year since the funeral. Why are you calling me?"

Return to Leiper's Fork

Chapter 3: The Crisis

Years had passed since the day Rachel told Jesse it was over forever. Rachel had not only attended prom with Randall but the two started dating. She had seen Jesse once, since graduation. Her relationship with Randall had grown and one night she found herself accepting a tiny diamond and agreeing to marriage, after the two graduated from college. Life was good, until Randall got sick and passed away. The next spring, she and several teachers lost their contract. Her world had simply fallen to pieces.

Rachel donned a dark, fuchsia silk skirt. Hastily, she snatched the matching top from its hanger. After applying her makeup to perfection, she smiled and fluffed her long brown curls. From her closet she selected dark heels. The new outfit she had recently purchased made her feel glamorous and she started humming as she reached for her shoes. She was glad she had polished her nails the night before, because the color set off her golden tan. Working on the back porch creating wreaths, did have advantages. She brushed her hair again for good measure and was glad the sun had highlighted her brown hair.

Two months before, she had signed a contract with a college to teach Art Appreciation, three nights a week. Times had been tough since Randall's death. There had been enough insurance to bury him but not enough to pay the monthly bills. Her parent's offer of money was immediately turned down and she had sent her resume to several high schools and colleges in the area. How she had prayed and hoped for a job. After several weeks, Human Resources called from a local college. Rachel felt fairly confident she had the experience and ability to get the position but didn't want to bet her tiny bank account on it. Mrs. Claremont had told her the art department was excited to have her application, especially with her being a graduate and an up-coming artist in the region. It had helped to place some of her work at Leiper's Fork Art Gallery on Old Hillsboro Road. Ms. Fox had been very encouraging and her small prints were selling well.

Mrs. Claremont asked if she'd enjoy working for the college and she'd remembered her response. "Yes! Oh, my! Yes!" Ecstatic, she'd immediately called her parents, who invited her to dinner to celebrate. Money would not be such an issue now but she'd still have to be thrifty in her spending.

Driving down the highway, she passed the prestigious home where Jesse's parents had lived. Steedmore! The large Greek Revival home with its massive columns and large porch set back from the road. The long drive seemed to beckon her toward the mansion.

"Jesse! It's impossible to dismiss you from my mind and it has been years. Every time I turn a corner, there's always something that reminds me of you. Why did you call me earlier and what are you doing in Leiper's Fork?"

As she passed the house, a van pulled into the driveway. Mumbling to herself, Rachel watched it slowly make its way down the long, black ribbon drive that ended abruptly at the back of the historic home. The house had been built on part of the original land grant given to Colonel Jesse Steed, after the Revolutionary War. Rachel remembered the tennis courts behind the house and the huge archway covered in purple wisteria that led to an outdoor pool. She and Jesse had played many a tennis game and swam in the long, rectangular pool during hot days. Afterward, Mrs. Steed had managed to appear at the right moment carrying a tray of sandwiches and tall glasses of tea.

Why, after all these years is a cleaning company coming to Jesse's house? He's not been home since the death of his parents.

The house and all of its contents had set since the tragedy, that not only reeled Leiper's Fork but all of Nashville. The accident had happened at the end of Rachel's senior year of college and Rachel recalled the incident as if it had happened yesterday. She'd been busily helping her instructor organize and store boxes of art supplies, after the last day of class. Her cell rang, as she lifted another box.

"Mom! I'm really busy. Is this an emergency?"

"Yes, honey. I wouldn't bother you if it weren't. Rachel, I need to let you know that Jesse's parents were killed yesterday. From what I know, he

Return to Leiper's Fork

flew in immediately from San Francisco and I'm trying to get food organized to take to his home. Is it possible for you to hurry home and help me? I've about got it ready but from what I understand, there will be quite a few relatives at his house. Bertha and I have been cooking all afternoon but I'd feel a whole lot better if you would come home and go with me. Please don't say you can't. I realize what this means to you but Jesse is grieving. Rachel, please say you'll help." Mrs. Locke waited a few moments, all the while biting her lip. "Honey, you do know I've been having trouble with my back and neck and I need help carrying those containers of food."

Rachel interrupted quickly, realizing her mother was up to her old tricks to get her way. "Mom, I'll be there as soon as possible. It shouldn't take too much time to deliver food. Jesse will be too busy to know we were even there. It's been four years since I've seen him. We've gone our separate ways, you know. Remember, I'm in love with your future son-in-law and there's a wedding being planned."

"Of course I didn't forget, honey. Just hurry home. I wanted to get the food there in time for dinner. I've already talked to one of Jesse's aunts and she said for us to drive to the back door. She'll be waiting to help us. She seemed real nice, too."

Later, a nervous Rachel tapped on the back door of the mansion. Boxes of pies and a large sliced ham, along with numerous salads, breads and large containers of sweet tea were soon set on the kitchen table. As she kicked the car door shut, Jesse appeared on the drive. A flutter of plastic and paper greeted him, as Rachel's hands flew into the air. As she whispered his name, he looked up in surprise. His steel, gray eyes were fixed on the young woman wearing a white summer blouse and faded jeans. Her thick mass of curls were held back by her dark sunglasses. Jesse remembered those wide brown eyes and thick dark lashes. Yes, it was Rachel he had seen from the wood. From embarrassment, both knelt to pick up the scattered paper goods and plastic utensils.

"Rachel! I . . . didn't expect to see you." Jesse studied the woman before him _ the one he'd not seen in four years. "You're prettier than ever, but I'm not the least bit surprised. You always were." Jesse quickly handed her the utensils and stood back with his hands on his hips.

Rachel bit her lip. "I didn't know if I'd see you or not Jesse but Mom needed help. I'm sorry about the way I look. I was at school putting up supplies in the art department and . . . ." Rachel looked down at her jeans and white eyelet top which revealed a bright orange stain. "I should have changed but we were bringing in the food and I didn't think I'd see anyone I knew." She looked at her feet and kicked a tiny pebble on the drive. "You look nice too, Jesse but you always did. I was always proud to be seen with you."

Rachel could not help but admire the handsome man in tan slacks and a yellow plaid shirt. She'd always admired his rugged looks but now he was quite striking. His dark hair had been bleached by the California sun and his skin was evenly tanned. She searched his hand for a ring but saw none. Evidently, Jesse was not married but she was weeks away from saying her vows.

Jesse reached out to her. "I'm glad you came. I just wish we'd met under happier circumstances. I can't believe what has happened." He blinked and looked down at her. He tried to hide his grief by laughing but a lump formed in his throat. She watched, as he swallowed several times. "I was getting ready to come home for a visit before settling into a job in San Francisco. Now, I'm not sure. Not sure about anything."

"Jesse." Rachel touched his arm. "I'm so sorry for your loss. If there is anything I can do, please don't hesitate to call. You'll always be a friend. Always, even if Randall and I . . . ." She reached out to him and their eyes met. As he searched her eyes, he seemed to penetrate her heart. Taking the paper goods from her hands he set them on the steps. It was then Jesse drew her toward him in a warm embrace. Tenderly he pressed her head against his chest, all the while whispering her name. His heart raced but he had no control over the moment.

"My little Rachel. My little Pork Princess of Williamson County. Those little pig ears they attached to your tiara were pretty cute." Rachel laughed, remembering she had won the pork industry contest. Jesse had been her date and had never forgotten that day. His shirt felt soft to her face, as tears slid down her cheeks. "Little porker, I'd better get my act together. I've never been religious and that was probably part of my problem but right now I'm desperate for help. I only hope I can make it through the next few days and weeks. This has been such a blow to me. I'll close up the house in a week and return to San Francisco but I'm not too sure what to do with all

Return to Leiper's Fork

this land. One day, I hope to come back to the area and settle down but it will be a while. I've always loved Leiper's Fork for several reasons and you're one of them regardless of what has happened between us. I ask your forgiveness for the things I said and the way I acted, especially after you let Benton take my place. Can you forgive me for my pride and stupidity and for not fighting to win you back? You were the best thing in my life and I lost you." Jesse shook his head in unbelief and wiped his eyes.

Before Rachel could nod her answer, a door slammed. "Honey, are you ready to get back to the house?" Rachel turned, as her mother stared at her and Jesse strangely. "I need to get back and get Dad's supper on the table. It's his night to host the trivia game."

Why is Jesse holding Rachel?

Jesse searched Rachel's face for some response but seeing none, whispered, "Thanks, Rachel. I'm glad you came." She handed him the utensils and as she drove away, a thousand thoughts filled her mind. She knew she loved Randall, even though the last four years had been tough with him working and going to school at the University of Tennessee. She had taken on a part time job at the college and worked hard to finish her own degree. In a few days, she would graduate and so would Randall. He'd been offered a job in Williamson County, as a new high school coach. Wedding plans were being made, and Randall hoped Rachel would stay home and start their family.

"Honey, my mom had to work and it was tough not only on her but on Dad and me. I'd like for you to continue painting and one day I'll build you the cabin you want. It's going to have a rhododendron balustrade and a studio. You need lots of light and lots of room. Being an artist has been your life time dream and I want you to be the happiest angel in the world. Imagine me, Randall Benton marrying the prettiest little woman in the state of Tennessee. My angel cannot only cook but is the best artist around. One day, all of the world will recognize her for her talent."

Rachel laughed. "Keep dreaming, Randall."

That August, before school started, Rachel received a contract to teach art in the local high school. Her excitement overflowed, as she waited for

Randall to arrive home. Seeing his frown, she held him close. "Randall, this is what I have prepared to do, sweetheart. Art is what I do best. I want to teach students everything I know." Randall gritted his teeth but true to his nature, told her he wanted only her happiness.

After three years, Randall began drawing plans for the cabin which would definitely include a studio and a limestone fireplace for his beloved Rachel and two years later, Randall was taken by ambulance to the hospital. After numerous tests at Vanderbilt, the diagnosis caught the couple by surprise. The graying specialist gazed at the two quietly and turned his eyes to his white starched jacket. After clearing his throat, he adjusted his glasses.

"It's what I suspected from the start and now I know for sure. Randall, it is pancreatic cancer, which means a malignant neoplasm of the pancreas. Only the Good Lord knows how much time you have but I like to be up front with all my patients. This type cancer is cruel and invasive.
You might have six to ten months at the most."

Randall gasped, as Rachel doubled over. Trying to maintain his composure, the patient gripped his wife's hand. "Son, if it had been caught earlier, you might have had five year but it's rare. We need to start some type of treatment, as soon as possible, if nothing else, for pain. Expect more jaundice and weight loss. You also need to quit your job. As a coach, you won't have the stamina to work because this monster will keep you constantly nauseated." Seeing their grief, he stood up. "Now, I'll leave you two alone but don't hesitate to call if you have questions." He walked out quietly and set an appointment for the man known in Leiper's Fork, as "Coach."

Randall and Rachel poured a lifetime of living into their marriage during those next months. Randall insisted they take a short trip to Florida but plans were changed at the last minute. Even short trips exhausted him. During the day, his mother stayed with him so Rachel could work and at night, Rachel and Randall held each other, knowing one day Rachel would be alone. Each moment would have to be cherished and Randall hid love notes all over the house knowing Rachel would find them when she most needed to know she was loved.

Jesse slowly descended the steps to the small coffee shop. He was fighting fatigue and knew the quarterly trustee's meeting at the college had lasted far longer than he had anticipated. He stood breathing in the aroma

Return to Leiper's Fork

of coffee, realizing the manager was sizing him up with her eyes. Her gaze followed him from the tips of his expensive loafers to his rugged attractive face. Jesse had flown into Nashville the night before and had been so exhausted, he'd tossed most of the night. The manager watched as he placed his dark rimmed glasses in their case and tucked it in his pocket.

Glasses are necessary for reading but aside from that, they're only a nuisance.

Continuing with great interest, the blond watched as the stranger raked his hands through his dark curling hair, exhaled, then stroked his jaw with his thumb. Slowly, he followed the coffee aromas to the front of the café.

Sophie continued giving the stranger an admiring glance. He was older than most of the students and certainly better dressed. She liked his crisp white shirt and the way he filled out his gray suit.

He surely must work out each week.

His face and arms were deeply tanned and she wondered what he did for a living. He was pure muscle and she liked what she saw. She noticed the sprinkling of silver in his dark hair and remembered many men were more attractive with gray hair. Twinkling eyes caught her glance and a smile appeared on the man's lips, as he approached her. Sophie placed her hands on her ample hips and pointed to the cups she had stacked near the coffee urns. She was glad she had applied fresh lipstick and lined her eyes with her new plum eyeliner. She pushed a strand of hair behind her ear and hoped she looked older than her nineteen years. She met his smile with one of her own.

"The coffee's still good, if you'd like a cup but there's one problem. After eight thirty, I give it away. I'll close in ten minutes."

A young woman sitting at a small table reading text messages, nodded and mumbled, "I don't need any more coffee. Thanks. I'm going to leave before you can say, "Monet." Not hearing a response, she looked up.

Sophie smiled in her direction, as she motioned the gentleman to select a coffee. "Miss! I was talking to this person. Sorry about that." Sophie pointed to the well-dressed man intently studying the different flavors.

"I'll take that one." He pointed to a Blue Mountain brand that promised a robust flavor. "Just black, please. No cream or sugar. I have a bit of a drive to make and I need to stay awake." His twinkling gray eyes traveled across the café to the woman dressed in fuchsia. "First, I need to talk to an old friend."

He walked quietly to the table, where a pale Rachel sat. He was reminded of the last time he had seen her _ the day of the funeral. How could he ever forget how she had looked _ more like death warmed over than a living person. Her face had appeared frozen, even in the summer heat and the sparkle in her eyes had died days before. She had fled, after he reached out to her _ when he wanted to console her. He left soon after that and after all those years, he could still hear her sobs. As Rachel looked up, her chocolate brown eyes were met by pools of warm gray. "Jesse! Wh . . . What are you doing here?" She checked her watch and stared wide eyed at the man who appeared as calm as a millpond on a hot summer afternoon.

"It's so late. What are you doing at this college? I mean, you can go anywhere you want." The longer Jesse stared at her, the more nervous she became. "I . . . I don't even know what I'm trying to say. I guess I'm flustered at seeing you."

Return to Leiper's Fork

Chapter 4: The Confession

"Rachel, I might ask you the same question. What are you doing up so late, and drinking coffee before your bedtime?" Jesse smiled and reached for his cup of coffee. He laid a twenty dollar bill in Sophie's hand, nodded at her and said, "Keep the change."

The manager slipped the bill into her jean's pocket and tried to remember where she had seen the gorgeous creature. Finally, the memory clicked. She had seen his picture on the front page of the student newspaper, that week. He had become the college's youngest trustee. How could she ever forget that beautiful smile and the dark hair that made his tanned face seem even more irresistible? There was one thing she never forgot _ a handsome face. Sophie remembered the article that mentioned a sizable donation and how he was following in his father's footsteps by serving as a college trustee. Yes, the college had found a savior and he was none other than, Mr. Jesse Steel or was it Steed? Under her breath she muttered, "Sophie girl, maybe you're setting the bar a bit high. One day your prince will arrive and whisk you out of this coffee bar, before you can say, 'Starbucks!' But with your luck, it won't be this handsome trustee."

Jesse pulled out a chair, despising the screeching sound it made on the wooden floor. "Rachel, I have come home for a little while. Even though I got my degree at San Francisco State and lived there, my heart will always be in Leiper's Fork. There is no place in all the world like Williamson County to lay my head."

Rachel nodded. "You're right. There's no place like Leiper's Fork and I was born there and I'm going to die there. That will always be my home and I'm never leaving. While we have a few minutes, tell me about your life in San Francisco."

Jesse exhaled, sipped his coffee and grinned widely. Rachel loved his smile. His eyes were sparkling. "I love it and I've had a wonderful life there, but I have some major business here. The old house needs some repairs but it's not something my trusty handyman can handle. I'm talking major overhaul. I've got some plans up my sleeve but what I'm more concerned about, is how you've been doing. Why are you out so late this evening? Did the coffee at The Country Store in Leiper's Fork run out? " Jesse chuckled and took another sip. He knew exactly why Rachel Benton was at the college.

Hesitating, Rachel spoke, "No Jesse, the coffee didn't run out there or at Puckett's Restaurant. It probably never will. Af . . . After Randall died, I had to find another job. Teaching contracts were cut and I lost my job at the high school. When I had given up hope, I got a call, to interview as an instructor for the Art Appreciation evening classes. It was truly a miracle. I'm not sure if being an artist helped. Maybe, being an alumnus got me the job but it was a gift from Heaven. I am so thankful I still get emotional when I talk about it." She blinked and smiled.

Jesse bit his lip wondering if he should say what his heart was begging him to say. At the same time, a voice cautioned him to keep silent. His heart won the battle. "Your tears are precious, Rachel. Always were, always will be . . . at least to me. " Jesse forced a smile, as he witnessed the quiet stare, of the woman beside him. Flustered, she looked down at her half-filled cup.

"I've probably embarrassed you but honesty is still the best policy, Rachel. At least that's what my father tried to drill into me." He laughed shyly. "Forgive me. I'd never intentionally do that and I'm glad you were offered a job here. It's a beautiful college."

Rachel sat in silence but after a few moments continued. "I wasn't the only one who lost their contract. It was rough for all of us who found ourselves without a job but to make matters worse, there wasn't much left after Randall's funeral." She looked up to see a flicker of surprise in Jesse's eyes. "I hope I'm not boring you with information you don't need, Jesse. Please forgive me. It must be later than I think, the way I'm babbling. I'd better go." She reached down to grab her purse.

"Please don't go, Rachel." Jesse looked around to see other students talking at their table and Sophie studying quietly at the bar. It was well past nine o'clock. His eyes returned to Rachel. "I would have helped you, if I'd only known. I'm so sorry for all you had to deal with."

Return to Leiper's Fork

Rachel grasped his hand, nearly knocking over the cup. "Jesse! I could never! I mean, I couldn't ask you to help me. I never told anyone. Besides, what would Susanna say? We're adults and we carry our own burdens." She laughed nervously, hoping no one was watching or listening.

"Jesse's eyes narrowed. "Susanna? Rachel, don't you know? Did you not hear about Susanna and me?"

"Yes, Jesse, I did. The last I heard was that you had married and you and Susanna were making your home in San Francisco. I believe that is where you live, isn't it? Will she be joining you at Steedmore, soon?"

Jesse slowly shook his head and gently rubbed his jaw. He gazed at her with eyes of steel, as a muscle twitched in his neck. "Rachel, we've been divorced for four years now. The marriage barely lasted twelve months. Sometimes I wonder how it lasted that long but I don't fault Susanna. Marriage to her wasn't what I'd always imagined marriage should be. After a while, she got tired of being alone and started traveling for weeks on end. I worked sixty to ninety hours a week and went home to change clothes and leave again. After a while, we just drifted apart and Susanna filed for divorce. It was a bitter sweet moment when I signed the papers but I gave her everything. I thought that would ease my guilty conscience." Jesse sat back in his chair and threw up his hands. "That's my story. I carry all the blame for the break up, because I did not love her when we married and why I agreed to all of it is beyond me. Maybe, in some cruel way, I hoped to get back at you for marrying Randall but I was my worst enemy."

Rachel silently mouthed the word, "divorce," as her cup dropped from her trembling hands. Brown liquid quickly spread like hot lava. Jesse grabbed napkins and began wiping the streams of brown streaming across the table. He held up one hand to Sophie, as she came running with a damp cloth. "It's okay. I've got it under control."

Rachel stood back in embarrassment . "Jesse! I'm such a klutz! Please forgive me. If I've ruined your clothes, I will pay to have them cleaned."

After wiping up the remains of the spilled coffee, Jesse spoke soothingly. "No harm done. Superman has saved the day or is it the night? Another beautiful woman has been rescued. You may thank me later, Lois

Lane." Both laughed, as Jesse continued drinking in the sight of the woman he had always loved _ the woman he had tried to forget. Little did she know the ashes he had tried so hard to bury, had burst into flames. Rachel blushed and looked away.

Maybe I can have another chance with Rachel.

Flustered, she grabbed her notebook. "It was nice Jesse and again, I apologize." Her eyes opened wide, when she noticed tiny, brown stains on his shirt. How did all that happen when she only meant to get coffee, check her email and drive home? Why did she tell Jesse about her lack of finances after Randall's death? Did he pity her now? Her lashes were wet, as she pushed back a lock of golden brown hair, hoping he had not noticed.

"Allow me, Lois Lane." Jesse pulled a small camera and a linen handkerchief from his pocket. Slowly, he dried her eyes.

"Jesse, I told you, I am a klutz. Now, you can believe me."

As he touched her face again, she reveled in the scent of his expensive cologne. He cupped her chin. "Missed one tiny tear, Rachel. Now, I need to thank you for making my day. I was feeling pretty lonely and tired before I came into the café." Jesse stuffed the handkerchief in his pocket and feasted his eyes on the stunning woman near him. He wanted to kiss her but knew better. He cleared his throat, picked up his camera and motioned her toward the door, as one of the students made his way toward them.

"Excuse me, sir. I saw your picture in the school paper and if I'm correct, you are our newest trustee." Jesse nodded. "I'm glad to meet you, sir. Would you like for me to take a picture of you and your wife? She is one heck of an art instructor."

Rachel flushed a deep pink and started to correct him but Jesse touched her lips with his finger. "We would love to have a photo, wouldn't we, darling? You can place it on your nightstand and when I'm away, you can dream of me. You know, a snapshot keeps a moment from running away, doesn't it, sweetie? We can always remember tonight, even if we're married a thousand years." Rachel forced a smile but Jesse felt her tremble when he wrapped an arm around her slender shoulders.

Afterward, she faced him with questions in her eyes. He only cocked an eyebrow and whispered huskily. "I'll see you to your car. Don't think a thing about what I said. I was just being nice. He didn't know I wasn't your husband. I didn't mean a word I said." After finding her car and reminding her to lock her door, he waved goodnight. Jesse couldn't help but wonder how it would have felt to press his lips to her moist pink ones and hold her trembling body next to his. Would her body have felt the same, as she felt before Randall Benton stole her away? No, Jesse knew as he stood alone watching the tail lights of her car blink in the darkness, her body would have been softer and her kiss would have tasted like rich wine _ wine sweetened by time.

Chapter 5- The Meeting

As Rachel rushed into the office the next evening, Mrs. Claremont, the receptionist, glanced at her and pointed to a man waiting across the hall. Softly, she whispered, "I hoped you'd be able to come in on your night off. Dr. Carter Viking is our newest hire and you'll be working directly with him. I wanted you to meet him and he insisted on waiting for you." Before Rachel could chide her, Dorothy Claremont, once a beauty but still striking in her sixties, called out to the dark haired gentleman dressed in a dark shirt and slacks. His clothing fit him as if it had been designed for his body.

Rachel turned to glimpse the man. As he approached, she noticed his thin dark mustache, and dark eyes with long lashes. His hair curled slightly and brushed the edge of his collar. Carter Viking was indeed a very handsome man.

"Dr. Viking, this is the assistant, who will be working with you. Rachel, meet your new boss, Dr. Carter Viking." Mrs. Claremont beamed, as the middle aged professor eyed the slim young woman wearing a white sleeveless dress. Her gold jewelry gave her a look of royalty.

The professor stretched out his hand, as he approached Rachel. He'd been wondering for weeks, what his assistant would look like and had been delighted after finding her picture with other staff photos. He thought she looked wholesome and innocent. He liked those qualities in a woman. He hoped she would not have to rush home each night to a husband. He had no reason to rush home. This move was the beginning of a new life. Together, he and Rachel could spend time implementing his new ideas for the art department and he knew it was going to be a pleasure working with her. Too many times in his career, he'd had the displeasure of working with females who scratched and clawed their way to the top and it didn't matter how many victims they left behind. Hadn't he recently left one in Arkansas? He nearly crooned, as he grasped her hand. "Please, call me, Carter. We'll be working closely, so let's dispense with the formalities and start out on a first name basis. Is that alright with you?"

Caught off guard, Rachel nodded and swallowed quickly. As she noticed

Return to Leiper's Fork

his stare, she grew nervous. What if she displeased him? What if he preferred to work with someone else instead of her? She needed this job_ needed it, desperately. "That is quite alright, Dr. Viking, I mean, Car. . . Carter."

"Well, that is settled. How about suggesting a place for dinner? Mrs. Claremont said you'd know the best place in Nashville to celebrate but only if you'd like to. You might have other plans but I hope not. I'm settled in my apartment but I am not a chef by any means and it has been a long day. I'd be pleased to talk about some of my plans, if you can go out with me. Frankly, I'm famished. I'm also without a car. I'll pick up my new one tomorrow, after it's been serviced. "

Rachel looked at Mrs. Claremont, who began to motion them out the door with her hands. "Dear, take Dr. Viking to Monell's. You know that delightful place down town. The food is to die for and I can't think of a better place to have a, "Welcome to Nashville," dinner. My mouth is watering thinking about it but I'd better get home and get out that pasta, I baked this morning. Harry will be as restless as a jack rabbit wondering when he's going to get his dinner. Tonight, he plays cards with the boys. By the way, Rachel, since Dr. Viking doesn't have a car and you know Nashville better than he, would you be willing to drive and show him some of the sights on your way to Monell's? The Parthenon would be a good start."

Dr. Viking, put his hand on Rachel's back and stepped out the door.
"Thank you so much for agreeing to spend part of your evening with me. I hope I have not inconvenienced you in anyway. I thought you could fill me in on the department and I could share some cutting edge plans I have. I think we could increase enrollment and bring a lot of attention to the college at the same time. Also, thank you for being coerced into driving. I'd hated to walk." He smiled broadly and placed his hand on her back.

Rachel laughed, "Don't worry about that. I'll enjoy hearing what you have to say, Carter. With you at the helm, I'm sure we have nowhere to go but up even though the college is quite well known in the world of academia." Both laughed and as Rachel drove, pointing out the Nashville sights, she knew she was going to enjoy working with Carter Viking. It never hurt to be on good terms with a boss as charming as this professor.

She wondered if he was married. It was hard to tell these days.

As she drove, Dr. Viking put Rachel at ease by telling her about his childhood days in Arkansas. "Mom and Dad purchased an old house on a few acres in the country and my brother and I did a lot of exploring. For a long time, we dug up bottles and broken dishes. On rainy days we'd camp out in the attic for hours at a time. Mom let us spend some nights up there but it was kind of spooky. There were a lot of old things left in the attic by past owners. Mostly junk, broken furniture and old curtains and such but someone had dabbled with paints. We found plenty tubes of dried up oils and a lot of brushes. It changed my life and especially the old canvas I found under the rafters. It was as dirty as all get out. It was a painting of an old mansion and snow was drifting all around it. It was beautiful. I kept it in my room for years and later had it framed. It kindled my love for art and one day, I knew what I wanted to do for a life time. I wanted to inspire others, the way some nameless person years ago, inspired me with that winter picture. I want children to learn to paint and make a canvas come alive. Their art can speak as well as an adult's. That's one plan I have for our college _ training children to become better artists. Summer classes, you know. Now, I've talked too much. Tell me about you."

Rachel laughed softly for a few moments then paused before answering. "My life in Leiper's Fork probably wasn't as exciting as yours but I wouldn't trade it for New York or Los Angeles. Oh! Here we are."

No one was as grateful as Rachel, as she spied the two story pink restaurant trimmed in white. An iron fence framed the property, which boasted lush green plants around a white sign, with tall purple painted iris. The restaurant reminded Rachel of a three layer strawberry cake with white icing much like the one at Joe Natural's Restaurant in Leiper's Fork. Her mouth watered thinking about the delicious confection. She pulled quickly into one of the last parking places. "Here we are. Food at last! My story will have to wait until later." She gave Carter a bright smile and waited until he opened her door and led her to the restaurant. "We are in for a wonderful treat, if you like pot roast, chicken and dumplings, Nashville's famous pulled pork or fried catfish. My mouth is watering right now, Carter. Thanks for inviting me and by the way, welcome to Nashville. It's called Music City, USA in case you didn't know. Every day will be an adventure."

Carter laughed and squeezed her shoulder lightly. This woman was not only a heart stopper but would be a pleasure to work with. He hoped again

Return to Leiper's Fork

she was not in a serious relationship or married. The last two years had taken its toll on him and he was glad to move on with his life. Carter took a deep breath and silently studied the woman standing so near him, he could smell her perfumed hair.

"A table for two, please." He smiled at the waitress, who quietly led them to a small corner table.

"Allow me, Rachel." Quietly, Carter seated Rachel then chose the chair across from her. He gazed quietly around the room. "Nice place. I think we'll enjoy this. I really didn't want Mrs. Claremont to drive me back to my apartment. I don't like to eat alone. Thanks for giving up your evening. I'll make it up to you one of these days."

"Well sir, you are very welcome. I didn't have a good reason for going home and I don't enjoy eating alone either. You'll find out in time, so I might as well tell you. My husband, Randall died a little over a year ago. We weren't blessed with children. I spend three evenings a week working at the college and I paint, not only to pass the time but it gives me a lot of pleasure to do something I love. Some of my work is featured in Leiper's Fork, where I live. It is a few miles from Franklin, which is below Nashville. You've probably never heard of it."

"Rachel, we're a lot alike, in many ways. I am a widower. When Mindy died, I was left alone and I thought I was going to lose my mind. She was carrying our first child. Finally, I had to move on. When I interviewed for this position, I knew it would be healthy for me. I needed a fresh start. I think I'm really going to enjoy Nashville. It's been wonderful so far, thanks to you. Maybe one day, you can show me Leiper's Fork. Did it get its name because someone named Leiper lost his fork?"

"No. It seems there was a fork in the stream and the people named it, after Mr. Leiper." They laughed together and Carter knew he was going to enjoy working with Rachel.

As soft music played in the background, Carter patted Rachel's hand. As she looked up to meet his gaze, he looked across the room and quickly withdrew his hand as if he had seen an apparition. As he raggedly sucked in his breath, she watched his face. Not knowing what to say, Rachel touched his arm and hoped he was not getting sick.

Carter shrugged his shoulders. "I'm sorry. I still have times when my wife's death hits me hard. I never know how I'm going to react. It's when I see someone that reminds me of her, that I nearly lose it." He pointed to a petite blond sitting at a table across the room. "That woman is a carbon copy of my wife." Carter ran his hand through his hair and breathed heavily. "Forgive me."

As Rachel turned to see the woman in question, the woman turned toward her. "Rachel! Rachel Benton! Good to see you again!" In seconds, the sophisticated Susanna Steed appeared at Rachel's table. A pale Carter stood, as she approached and reached out a trembling hand. Surely he was seeing his wife's ghost.

"Carter, this is Susanna Steed. Susanna, Dr. Carter Viking, our new professor. He arrived today and I'll be working with him." Rachel wondered what Susanna would say but it didn't take long for Susanna to grab the attention of the handsome but pale professor.

"It's been years, since I left Leiper's Fork. I've been living in San Francisco and travel a lot. I got engaged yesterday and I have to show off my fabulous ring." She held out her well-manicured hand and giggled, as the stone flashed brilliantly in the soft candle light. Carter paled even more as his hands trembled violently.

Rachel's eyes feasted on the huge, pear-shaped diamond on Susanna's well-manicured finger as Susanna gushed, "I can't believe, how happy Jesse has made me. I'm the happiest woman ever. Never knew how to cook but the second time around, I will learn. Jesse is going to join us soon. I think he got delayed but that's Jesse. All work and no play makes for a dull boy." She laughed. "However, I'm glad to meet you Dr. Viking. Bye, Rachel." With those parting words, Susanna rejoined the two men at her table. Rachel, reeling from the news braced herself by gripping the table's edge.

How can this be?

"Are you okay, Rachel?" Carter watched Rachel's face pale, as she reached for a glass of water. Angry thoughts filled he.

So Jesse Steed and Susanna are remarrying. Funny, he never told me, he got engaged.

Return to Leiper's Fork

"Carter, Susanna and I graduated together from Hillsboro High. She moved to California to attend college. San Francisco State, I believe. She was never a close friend of mine but it was kind of her to drop over and speak." She took another sip of water hoping to control her emotions.

Susanna never changed. She drops words like bombs, creating destruction all around her. You would think the woman had a conscience but then, she never did.

"She's very striking but she can't hold a candle to you." Carter's smile died, as footsteps ended at his table. When Rachel looked up, she choked.

"Rachel, are you, okay?" The man patted her back firmly, as she coughed and sputtered. Heads turned in their direction.

"I . . . I'm okay, Jesse. Just got a drop of water down the wrong pipe." Concern was written on Carter's and Jesse's face but Jesse's also reflected jealously.

"You gave me cause for concern, Rachel. I wouldn't want anything to happen to you." Jesse smiled at Carter and reached out his hand. "I'm glad to see you again, Dr. Viking. I'm an old friend of Rachel's."

"Yes, I remember you. I could have helped Rachel but you were in the right spot at the right time. Thanks for intervening."

Ignoring him, Jesse tilted Rachel's chin with his hand. "Are you okay, princess?"

Quickly, she brushed his hand away. "Quite okay Mr. Steed. Please don't let me keep you from your party. I'm sure Susanna is missing you. By the way, congratulations. You certainly have your work cut out for you _ again."

Jesse looked confused. Rachel might well have slapped him. "I didn't think anyone knew. I only made my decision yesterday and we're signing the legal documents tonight. Did you talk to Susanna?"

37

Rachel took two breaths and shuddered. "I heard Jesse and I'm happy for you. I was surprised, that's all." Rachel turned to Carter, as Jesse's eyes clouded with disbelief. How did news travel so quickly?

"I'd like to talk to you soon, Rachel. I'll call. Right now I'm in an important meeting." He checked his Rolex. "In fact, I have held them up. I was just walking in when you started choking. But as far as I'm concerned, you're much more important than a meeting." Carter's eyes glittered, as Jesse searched Rachel's face. Did he see hurt in her eyes? He hurried to his table, where the other two huddled over a pile of papers.

"So you know Mr. Steed, Rachel? Not that it is any of my business." Carter unfolded his napkin.

"He's someone I used to know, Carter. It's all in the past and has been for years. Let's enjoy our dinner." Though Rachel forced a smile Carter felt their friendly camaraderie had been strained by Jesse's sudden appearance. Their dinner was eaten in silence. Afterward, Rachel drove him to his apartment. Jesse Steed had ruined her evening.

Later that night, Rachel's doorbell rang. As she opened her door, she couldn't believe she saw Jesse standing there. Acid rose up in her throat, as she remembered her conversation with Susanna. "Jesse! It's late _ really late."

"Rachel, it won't take me long to say what I need to say. I know it is late. I've had a very long day." Wearily, he leaned against the door and in the twilight, Rachel could see lines of exhaustion on his face. He had loosened his tie and turned the cuffs to his shirt. Sighing deeply, he groaned, "Rachel, what has happened?"

Not sure if to feel sorry for herself or for him, she responded tiredly.
"Jesse, I'm not sure what you're talking about. Nothing has happened but you need to leave."

"Rachel, I wanted to see you. I need to warn you of someone. I had to come." He tilted her chin and pulled her close.

Rachel pushed with a force, she didn't know she possessed. "No Jesse! I don't need to be warned of anything or anyone. It's crazy for you to come here. It's over between you and me and has been for a long time. Go! And

Return to Leiper's Fork

by the way, you have a new life or did you forget?"

At her words, Jesse's eyes flashed. "Forget what, Rachel? That you don't mean anything to me? You loved me once and you knew it when you married Randall. Why did you go through with it, Rachel? Why?" He reached out again to draw her near and felt the sting of her slap. His hand flew to his cheek. "Wh . . . What are you doing? What have I done to hurt you? Everything I've done lately has been for you."

"Including your engagement to your former wife? I'm not your plaything, Jesse. You can't love a woman and run to another." Rachel pushed against him and fled into her bedroom. Throwing herself across the bed, she cried out for the husband who could not help her. Jesse rapped on the door calling her name but his effort proved fruitless. She had locked the door. After a while he shook his head, kicked the post on the porch and stumbled off to his car. His mission had failed. Slowly, he drove down the lane and entered Old Hillsboro Road. After a few moments, Steedmore loomed before him and the rambling mansion had never looked so huge and so foreboding.

That night, he lay in his bed feeling confused and lonely. Had he made a mistake in inviting Susanna to come to Leiper's Fork? Would he find happiness again, or had he made the biggest mistake of his life? Time would surely tell but now, Carter Viking was a threat. Jesse knew Carter's background but only wanted to share a few things with Rachel, who refused to hear him. Miserably, he tossed and turned, waiting for a shaft of sunlight to flood the darkness that filled hi world.

What did Rachel mean when she insinuated I was engaged to Susanna? Has she lost her mind? Grief does strange things to people but I thought she would have been over the worst of it by now.

Chapter 6: The Romance

"I hate you Jesse Steed! Hate you forever!"

Weeks had passed, since the night Rachel slammed the door on Leiper's Fork newest entrepreneur. Now giant trees which had stood for centuries had crashed to the ground and been hauled away. Ancient stone walls that had stood in the hot sun and been home to field mice for years had been pulled down one by one and placed in piles for future use. The fertile rolling hills that boasted tons of hay each summer had been transformed into huge piles of dark brown earth. Gigantic caverns had been cut into the soil and Rachel looked at the heavy earth moving equipment in disgust. She remembered her vow to Randall and after witnessing the destruction, her vow was strengthened. The landscape of her beautiful Leiper's Fork was scarred and it was all Jesse's fault. She had vowed to fight him and she would.

The residents of Leiper's Fork spent evenings discussing the hundreds of acres that had seen no change in their life time. Now, with all the activity, the talk centered on what Jesse was going to build. The usual conversations about the weather and tourists had been forgotten in the light of new construction.

"Harold, I'm telling you now, that Jesse is building a new subdivision and that's that!" Harley stroked his moustache and squinted at his neighbor, who was also eyeing him.

"Well that's yore view, Harley Dobbins but I'm telling you, the boy has sold us out and he's gonna put cattle in there. Looks like a big barn is being built and that hole in the ground spells nothing but a pond, where he's gonna git his water. I've lived long enough to know a pond and a barn when I see one and I ain't a lying. Don't make me git up outta this chair to show you I mean business." Slowly, Harold spat a stream of dark tobacco so expertly it landed in the empty eight ounce can near his chair.

"Can you two quit your arguing long enough to have a piece of this peach cobbler?" Mary Mayberry carried two plates of warm pie out to the men, who suddenly seemed more interested in dessert than what was

Return to Leiper's Fork

happening on Jesse's land. "Kind of nice to have a little peace and quiet in the evening now, ain't it?" Mary looked at her husband and winked. Seems all he was interested in lately was what was happening down the road at Little Jesse's. Even though Jesse Steed was a grown man, she couldn't call him by any other name. "Well, let me tell you boys something. If Little Jesse does anything, it will be right good. That's always been true of him. So, expect something wonderful regardless of what it is." Grabbing her husband's arm she announced loudly, "Harold, it's gitting to be past your bedtime, don't you think? Lights have been out at Country Boy's and Puckett's a long time now. The streets are deserted and everybody's gone home and gone to bed, while you two geezers are arguing about what's being built down the road." She padded inside the large pink home that had stood on the edge of Old Hillsboro Road as long as she could remember. She'd been born in this house and this was where she would live and die.

Rachel stood quietly at the back of the auditorium. Her friendship with Carter Viking had grown and today, she watched the popular professor instruct his students. When Carter noticed her, he smiled and waved. He was proud of the beautiful woman with the heart shaped face and full red lips. Today, she had styled her hair in a loose chignon. Her face was pink from the attention she was receiving and her brown eyes sparkled. A smile played on her lips. Dressed in a white sleeveless blouse and black fitted skirt, Rachel was a lovely sight to see. He admired her tanned body and how she looked so striking in such simple clothing. "Students, you never know who is going to pay a visit and I'm glad Miss Benton is here. I believe you all know our Art Appreciation instructor, Miss Rachel Benton." Heads turned and Rachel, conscious of their scrutiny waved and backed out the door. "I need to meet with you later, Miss Benton," said Carter. She nodded.

Am I in love with Carter? I think he is in love with me but I don't want to rush things. Randall has only been gone a year and I can't rush into anything. And if I wanted to, I can't forget what Jesse said.

What had he meant when he said he needed to warn her of someone? She hurried to her office and selected her DVD for her evening class. Anxiously, she looked over her notes but she kept seeing Jesse's tired face when he appeared that night at her home.

The rumor was Jesse had left for Seattle and lost everything in the most recent stock market plunge. The gossip ran through town faster than water in Leiper's Creek during a thunder storm. The wealthy Jesse Steed, descendent of Colonel Jesse Steed was broke and Rachel was glad. She hoped he'd never have a dime for another plane ticket, much less destroy the farms around Leiper's Fork.

A sign was soon placed near the construction site, stating that the JHR Corporation was the owner and developer of the land. Evidently, Jesse had lost his shirt and fled Leiper's Fork from embarrassment. If he returned, he might find Rachel had married Carter Viking. She couldn't wait to share her life and love of art with the talented visionary who was taking Nashville by storm. Already he had established weekend art classes for children and there was a waiting list for parents who knew for a certainty they had a child prodigy.

After class, Rachel had coffee with Carter in the café. "You know I am beginning to fall for a certain art instructor." Carter smiled tenderly and grasped her hand warmly.

Instinctively, she pulled her hand away and whispered, "Carter! You and I both could lose our jobs. You know the rules about dating staff. You can't romance me in front of these students."

"I'm sorry, Rachel. I didn't think I could go another minute without touching the prettiest woman in Nashville. I'd always heard southern women were beautiful but you captured my heart before I had time to look around."

"Carter, did you fall in love with someone after your wife's death? I mean, I know it has only been a short while but I'm curious. Maybe, jealous." Rachel watched Carter closely. How would he react to her question?

Carter chuckled. "No! Not really. There's certainly no one to be jealous of. There was a woman I worked with and we dated a while but it was over when I moved here. She was a dean of a college _ an artist. I dated her for various reasons but decided to move on with my life and that is how I ended up here. Now, it's not worth our time to talk about her. She's gone and forgotten." He sipped his drink and wiped his moustache slowly.

Return to Leiper's Fork

Rachel leaned toward him. "Carter, I have a lot to do before the weekend is over. In fact, I'm painting for most of it. You see, I've been invited to exhibit some of my paintings in Nashville. Dealers and collectors are coming from across the nation and I'm so excited. One of my best pieces was painted after Randall died. It's entitled, *The Promise*. I painted almost four days nonstop. I was told to put a price on each piece and Lisa, the owner of Leiper's Creek Art Gallery, where I placed some of my art, said she would help me. I'm still giddy about being asked."

Carter leaned forward, after looking around to see if anyone was watching or listening. "Before you leave tonight, I want you to promise one thing. Promise me, you will love me forever and one day become my bride." He smiled and touched her ring finger. He noticed Rachel had removed her wedding rings.

"Carter! I have to think about it. We've only known each other for a short while and I never jump into things quickly. Yet, I do admire you."

"I hope it is more than mere admiration, Rachel. I hope it is love."

"I can't rule that out, Carter. I have developed feelings for you and one day soon, I hope to tell you how much I care."

"I'll be waiting, honey. Waiting day and night to hear you say the words I want and need to hear. I don't want to rush you but I'm lonely. I've been lonely for two years. I'd give you the world if you'd say you'll marry me."

Rachel bit her lower lip. Had she not heard similar words from Jesse, years ago? After a few months of dating, he had reached down to kiss her and nuzzle her cheek. "If you will marry me, I will give you Leiper's Fork and lay it at your feet."

She'd laughed but Jesse's eyes were serious. "I'm serious Rachel. I've watched you for a while. You're different from the other girls. There is something wholesome about you and one day I want us to marry. I know we're young but I know what I want. I only hope you want me as much as I want you. My goal is for you to become Mrs. Jesse Steed and I know I don't deserve you but I'm going to try."

Rachel's heart pounded and goose bumps covered her arms as she remembered Jesse's promise. Carter looked at her strangely and gently stroked her arm. "Darling, your arms are covered in goose bumps. In fact you're shivering. What's wrong?"

"Carter! It is just something I remembered. A man I cared for promised me long ago he would give me Leiper's Fork." She laughed nervously. "We parted over some silly argument. I married Randall and pushed that man to the far recesses of my mind. We went on with our lives. In fact he remarried his former wife. I'm Leiper's Fork. His wife is Paris, Rome and Vienna all mixed into one. I am a moth and she is the rare exquisite butterfly every man longs to possess. But that is in the past and it's over."

"No honey, I think you are the rare exquisite butterfly and I'm so glad I found you. Thank goodness, that man has been forgotten."

As Carter walked Rachel to her car, he huskily whispered, "Dream of me and I'll dream of you." As she looked up to accept his kiss, the face that blurred before her was not Carter's.

Jesse! Why won't you leave me alone? You torment me, when I'm not even near you.

Return to Leiper's Fork

Chapter 7: The Reunion

That week, Rachel painted the backdrop for her tenth high school reunion. Graduates would be returning and each person on the committee wanted to make sure the reunion was the best by far. The theme for the reunion was, *Dancing Through Life* and the theme song was, *I Hope You Dance*.

Rachel painted scenes of couples dancing through time and the committee laughed at the sketch of Roger Rabbit, Cotton Eyed Joe and the Electric Slide. Several had been practicing, the Jitterbug and the Mashed Potato. They had hired a DJ from Nashville and there was talk of, "Elvis," making a special appearance. Food was catered from several restaurants and the barbeque pork that oozed with smoky sauce was certainly to be a hit.

Barney Fife's police car had been cleaned and waxed and was waiting at the city limits to welcome all of the alumni to town. Dancing in the Fork would bring back memories and every man in love would be waiting to dance under the night time sky, until the band quit or his partner fell asleep on his shoulder. Jaunts to Garrison Creek Loop had been planned and a new contest named, From Frog to Prince, was sure to be a success. The local shops were full of treasures which would appeal to everyone who wanted to take home a reminder of their reunion. Musicians would be appearing at the Lawn Chair Theatre and antique dealers were getting in on the excitement. Politicians were ready with handouts and anxious to pump every hand in town.

Mrs. Sweeney's Bed and Breakfast had filled up months ago, and Anne, owner of the unique Moonshine Hill Inn, whispered that the two-story wood and stone cabin had been rented for a full week. She had free tickets to the concerts at Puckett's and had purchased plenty of Hillbilly Blend coffee for her guests. Alumni told her they wanted to leave their stress at the door and relax near her massive fireplace. They had plans to walk part of the twenty-two acre farm which at one time had been the center of an illegal moonshine operation. She claimed when she bought the land that it had been a dump but now it was paradise and some of the alumni were ready to experience it." Some were planning to visit the organic restaurant and make purchases from the homeopathic pharmacy. In all, the graduates were looking forward to returning to their hometown and having a fun filled weekend. Even the mayor had a proclamation for the alumni and city fathers had hung a welcome banner across Old Hillsboro Road. Everything was in order for all the graduates _ except the one not returning.

As Rachel touched up the panels and set them in place, Betsy folded the last napkin and sat down to rest her weary feet. Rachel raised her tired arms and rubbed her aching neck. "Betsy, do we have a lot of alumni returning this year?"

"Quite a few, Rachel. Only one emailed his regrets but you know the guy much better than anyone else."

"Who are you talking about, Betsy?" Rachel looked strangely at her best friend, who was filing a broken nail. Betsy Burdette had always been a beauty and she and Rachel had been friends since first grade.

"Don't give me that innocent look, Rachel Benton." Betsy laid down her file and pretended to peer into a crystal ball. "Oh, yes! I see a tall handsome man, you dated and I do believe his name is _ ah, can it be _ Jesse Steed?" Betsy burst out laughing.

Rachel drummed her fingers on the table. "Betsy, I don't really care if Jesse comes or not. That is all in the past and we're adults now. Our lives have gone in different directions. I guess his big concern is keeping his job in Seattle. You know people talked about him losing everything he had but that happens pretty frequently. Remember the recent scandal? At least Jesse wasn't the only one but can't say he didn't deserve it. I said I'd save Leiper's Fork if it killed me but now I think I will live and not have to eat radishes the rest of my life." She spread her arms in the air. "Ta- Dah!" The women broke into hysterics as Rachel held a broom on her shoulders pretending she was wearing a gown made from green velvet curtains. She was Scarlet O'Hara in, *Gone with the Wind.* Little did Betsy know, she also felt like Scarlet.

"There ain't nothing from the outside that can lick any of us." Rachel fanned her face speaking in her most southern accent. "Death, taxes and childbirth. There's never any convenient time for any of them. I think I will

Return to Leiper's Fork

just eat another radish and fade out of sight and when I do, Rhett Butler, you're going to be very, very, sorry." She laughed and pretended to pout.

Betsy clapped her hands. "Funny, funny girl. Rachel, you should have been an actress instead of an artist. By the way, is Carter coming with you to dance away the evening?"

Rachel shook her head in disappointment. "No! He told me he had to make a trip back to Little Rock to tie up some business. Something, about a lot of loose ends. I hated that he could not come but remember he owns a large house there. Maybe one day I'll get to see it."

After applying her makeup carefully that evening, Rachel twisted her hair into a loose chignon and carefully stepped into a fitted gold dress. She slipped her feet into gold strapped heels that felt so good they might as well been designed just for her. Her only accessories were pearl earrings and a small pearl bracelet. Even her brown eyes appeared larger as she smiled into the mirror. "That new mascara was exactly what I needed, and with Jesse not attending, I won't have to be so conscious about it."

After the dinner, each classmate was given a few minutes to tell about their life and what they had done in the last years. Some lived as far as Alaska and some had never moved away. That included Rachel. Leiper's Fork would always be her home and nothing could ever make her leave _ not even a man. Some were successful in the business world and some felt they were successful staying home to raise a family. A few had changed and some looked the same. Even Sid, the high school coach looked quite different, as he lovingly held his pregnant wife on the dance floor. His once full head of red hair was much thinner now and as the couple moved closer to Rachel, he paused to give her a peck on the cheek.

"You're just a beauty, Miss Rachel. Good to see you smiling, tonight."

Rachel sat alone, but not because she couldn't fill up a dance card. Her feet were screaming to shed the new shoes with each passing hour. Glamorous shoes didn't necessarily mean comfortable shoes. When she could stand it no longer, she strode barefoot to the front steps of the building. While carrying a soft drink, she hummed to the music and lifted her head to the sky. As if to thank her for her attention, a flash of light appeared in the darkness and zoomed eastward.

"Oh! The loveliness of God's creation." Rachel continued watching the streak of light then located a few constellations, bright specks against the backdrop of black velvet. Afterward, she retreated to one of the rocking chairs, which had been placed on the spacious porch. How she loved them..

A porch is always the soul of a building.

Footsteps sounded and she hoped it wasn't Willard, a man who had invited her to dance more than once. She was not interested in spending an evening with someone she didn't care to be with. She would be glad when Carter returned. He said he was bringing a gift and she wondered what it was.

"Make a wish on a falling star and it might come true." Rachel jumped, and turned to see the silhouette of a man against the bright auditorium. She watched as he made his way toward her. Only one man wore that expensive cologne and her heart raced as he knelt beside her. "I understand that stars put on a show for the most beautiful woman around. Surely that woman is you."

Rachel hesitated, as her heart beat wildly. She remembered his voice. She'd remember it if she lived to be a hundred years old. It reminded her of velvet _ soft, smooth. Although Jesse had left Leiper's Fork years ago, he had not lost his Tennessee accent. Tonight, his voice was magic.

"Jesse! You scared me to death. I thought no one would find me out here. I could only stand so much food and music. Guess I needed some peace and quiet."

"Betsy told me you were on the porch. I didn't know if you needed rescuing from a friendly bear or some lonely alumnus who's had too much sweet tea to drink." He laughed. "What a day! However, if you need rescuing from that moth there, I can gladly sweep you out of that rocker and hold you in my arms." He pointed to a bright green Luna moth which landed on the arm of her chair. As he sat down next to her, the startled moth flew quietly away.

"But I thought you . . . weren't going to be here. Betsy told me you were in Seattle working." She hugged her arms and shivered, conscious of

Return to Leiper's Fork

the man dressed in a dark suit and crisp white shirt. Jesse was more handsome than she had ever seen him. His dark hair glistened in the moonlight and his gray eyes sparkled as they met hers. A smile played on his lips as he offered a questioning glance. She watched, as he caressed her shoulder. He wanted to hug her but drew back and as the music floated from the auditorium, she shivered again. Jesse Steed was consuming her with his eyes. She blushed, as they listened to the lyrics of a song which suggested dancing because Rachel was afraid her heart would betray her. He was a married man who had evidently come without his wife and she was in love with Carter.

Jesse pressed closer. "Why aren't you in with the others? Dancing, I mean. A woman as beautiful as you should have a full dance card and be in the arms of every available man here tonight." Jesse gently caressed her arms. Rachel tried not to drown in the pool of dark gray that was sending messages to her heart _ messages she did not want to acknowledge.

"Why did you return, Jesse? You left months ago. Surely you did not come this far just to attend a high school reunion."

Jesse smiled, as his hand trailed up her shoulder. "Let me ask you a question in return. Why are you here without the famous Dr. Viking? I suppose he is busy painting some masterpiece in Arkansas or visiting one of his many loves. And speaking of masterpieces, has he painted your portrait yet? Surely you wouldn't turn down an offer to pose for such a famous artist would you, Rachel? Who wouldn't want to paint the lovely Rachel Benton?" Jesse's eyes mocked hers, as he touched her lips with the tip of his finger. "So soft _ so delicate. I've never forgotten them, Rachel _ never will." His voice died to a whisper, as he gazed into eyes that reminded him of a deer caught in the headlights of a car.

"How dare you, Jesse! How dare you say anything against that man! He might be older but he knows how to treat a woman. That's something you need to learn. Carter has been the perfect gentleman and he treats me like a lady. You are lying about him and you know it. Now answer my question. Why did you return to Leiper's Fork? Really! There's nothing here for you anymore and that includes me." Rachel took deep breaths wondering how she had been so bold.

Jesse's smile died as he rubbed his eyes. "Forgive me Rachel. I had no right to say what I said. I'm speaking out of pure exhaustion and I've been irritated all day. As far as my return, I've asked myself that question a thousand times. Maybe I left something valuable behind. I still don't have a real answer. Maybe one day, but not now. I work, eat and sleep. That has been my routine and although I don't really enjoy it, as much as I should, it's something I have to do to keep sane. It's lonely but I can deal with it. But we don't want to spend this lovely evening talking about me when the music is telling us to dance." He reached out his hand hoping with all his heart she would accept. He would have fought a grizzly bear for one opportunity to hold the beautiful woman dressed in gold.

Rachel remembered Jesse had lost his fortune. She supposed Susanna was wearing her clothes more than once, since there was little money in the Steed household. Talk was, she had also lost the land she had inherited and the JHR Corporation had gobbled it up. For once, Susanna had to live like other women who weren't born with a gold spoon in their mouth.

Rachel held up her hand, as Jesse stepped forward. Her voice was almost a whisper. "Jesse, I heard that you experienced some hard times when the stock market took a plunge. I just want you to know I am sorry it happened. What are you doing in, Seattle?"

Without hesitating, he replied, "Pumping gas." He stood back to watch the expression on her face.

Rachel gasped as her hand automatically covered her mouth.

"Jesse. I can't believe you're doing that type of job. Now, I didn't say it isn't honorable work but you know what I mean. I'm just surprised, that's all. Pumping gas, did you say?"

Jesse placed his hands in his pockets. "Money doesn't mean much to me anymore, Rachel. Life and happiness isn't about that. Couldn't you love a man who's broke?"

Rachel shook her head. So the gossip was true. Jesse had lost his fortune.

"You loved a man who didn't have a dollar to his name. You even married him." Jesse reached out to hold her. For some strange reason he

Return to Leiper's Fork

needed to feel her in his arms. "Couldn't you do it again?"

"No, Jesse. You can't do this. It's not right."

"Not right? What's not right, Rachel? What's right is that we are together and the long wait in the airport today was worth it. My flight was cancelled and I had to leave my luggage and have it delivered to the house but I got here before the night was over. It was worth it to see you, if you believe it or not. You are my beautiful gift tonight _ all dressed in gold. My beautiful golden girl." He pulled her to him again. "You and me, Rachel. Together, again." He pressed his lips against hers but only for seconds before Rachel wrestled from his embrace.

"No! That's not the way it's meant to be, Jesse. Do I need to remind you that you don't have the right to act like this? You have made your life in Seattle. I hope you're happy."

"Well, I might be, if I had the right woman with me." Jesse planted his hands on his hips and stood as rigid as the post holding up the porch. As he searched her face, he drank in the sight of the woman he had traveled so far to see. "Yeah, the right woman and she just happens to be you."

Rachel felt as if the air had been sucked out of her lungs. Turning, she pointed her finger inches from his handsome face. "You ought to be ashamed talking like that, when you are a married man. Men, today, don't know the meaning of the word, commitment. They can't wait to get a woman to the altar, then begin chasing someone new. If you think for one minute you've caught me, you're dead wrong. I'm a Christian and as difficult as it is to live the Christian life now days, I'm holding out for a Godly man. I'm not going to be unequally yoked to a man who will make my life miserable after the honeymoon or later. That may sound strange to you, Jesse but it is straight from my heart and I'm waiting for the Christian man who will love me and give me the family I've always wanted. I'm holding out if it takes a life time. The man, who marries me, will be the man I will love forever." Licking her dry lips, she looked into his face and spoke above a whisper. "Marriage to me is forever, Jesse and I am worth it, you know." She punctuated her last six words as she fanned her face with one hand.

Jesse's voice was husky. "Yes honey, you are. You definitely are worth it."

Tears stung her eyes and as she reached to wipe them, she saw a smear of mascara on her hand. Jesse would laugh at her for sure but she wasn't staying around to hear him.

Turning she stumbled but strong arms caught her. In a ragged breath, Jesse spoke. "Not so fast, Rachel! Did I understand you right? What do you mean I am a married man? If I am, I'd sure like to meet the woman I married. I'm tired of cooking, doing my own cleaning and coming home to an empty apartment every night. Thank God for work every day. Imagine all this time, I've been married and didn't know it." He laughed angrily then turned Rachel toward him. "Don't try to run away from me as you once did. I won't let it happen again and I shouldn't have allowed it then. You've always loved me and I've always loved you. Doesn't that count for something? It's time for explanations and I've got all night, so spill it out. I am worth it, you know." His eyes pierced hers before he smiled. Had he not heard her say those same six words earlier? Jesse draped an arm around her shoulders and gently led the bewildered woman to the time worn steps. "Let's sit over here. I don't want to miss one word. I am worth it, you know" He pulled her closer.

Rachel looked at him as though she had seen an apparition. "I didn't make it up, Jesse. I saw the ring and Susanna said you had made her the happiest woman in the world." Rachel choked out the next words slowly and bent her head. "She . . . even said . . . she was going to learn how to cook the second time around. So there!" Rachel searched his face and nervously twisted her fingers. "I'm an artist, Jesse but I'm not so creative I make up things like that. If you need a witness, ask Carter. He heard Susanna at Monells that night. And you! You were standing at our table. You two were together. What else was I to think?"

"Rachel, how can I forget that night? I was wishing I was the man with you, instead of Carter Viking."

Anger filled her. "Then, Mr. Business Man, give me your version of the story. If you did not marry Susanna, who did?"

Jesse looked at the woman facing him. If looks could kill, he'd already be dead. As he began laughing, tears rolled down his cheeks. "Rachel!" He

Return to Leiper's Fork

continued laughing until she put her hands on his shoulders and shook him.

"I cannot believe you thought I would ever marry that selfish woman again. What a fool I would have been, to make the same mistake twice. I wouldn't marry Susanna if she was the only woman in the state of Tennessee and the other women were on the moon." His laughter echoed into the darkness and Rachel didn't know if to laugh from relief or kick him in his shins for all she had suffered.

Jesse is not married. All this time, I assumed . . .

Jesse reached for his handkerchief and wiped his eyes. "If for no other reason, this conversation was worth my long trip. I haven't laughed this hard since we put the goat on top of the water tower for a senior prank." Shaking his head, he chuckled. "You are a creative woman. Lovely, I confess but I never dreamed you'd ever believe that. I think Susanna gave you enough rope to hang you. She was up to her old tricks and she knew how I've always felt about you. She's the jealous type but don't worry about her. She married an Italian artist and lives in Rome. I think he became interested in her when he saw how she could advance his career. He's five years younger but she has money and is quite beautiful. Needless to say, he has no money and that is why she bought her own ring. I do hope she learns to cook because after her money is gone, she'll be married to a starving artist. I hope she stays away from Leiper's Fork until we can discover if Mona Lisa was a man or a woman. There are questions about her or him, you know." He pulled the wide-eyed woman against him and held her until she whispered for him to release her.

"Jesse, what we had is over. Please let me go." To hurt him, she whispered, "Regardless of what you said, I still love Carter."

Rage surged through Jesse. As he clenched his teeth, his temples throbbed. "Then, if you really love him I hope he takes good care of you. Personally, I don't think you know who you love, Rachel. Knowing what I know about Carter Viking, I'd bet he holds his paintbrush tighter than he holds you. He's made up for a lot of things since . . . well, I won't go there." Jesse bit his lip and continued feasting his eyes on the woman he had lost _ possibly forever. Boldly, he continued. "You said you wanted the man God has for you. I don't think Carter is the man you're talking about. I know a lot about him but I don't have the liberty to tell you what I know. There were questions about him that couldn't be answered before we granted him an interview. I guess, Miss Benton, there are some things you will have to find out by yourself and I hope you wake up before it is too late. You're a Christian. Maybe you'd better have a little talk with God before things get too serious between you and Carter. Don't want you to be miserable after the honeymoon and if you marry him I'm afraid you might find yourself alone many nights and many weekends. Carter's like a tomcat, Rachel. He has to prowl. You don't have to believe me but I hope you're a little wiser after tonight." He took her arm. "I've got to leave. I've been up since five o'clock and I could sleep standing up." He took the arm of the woman too stunned to move and turned toward the lively group in the gymnasium.

After waiting for Rachel to retrieve her purse, he led her to her car. Her mind whirled with Jesse's words and her hands trembled as she placed her key in the ignition. Was Jesse telling the truth or saying things to turn her against Carter? Jesse bent down and leaned on the open window. "Good night, Rachel and goodbye. I hope you enjoy the rest of the reunion weekend. I'm flying back to Houston tomorrow, and then on to Seattle. Good luck, honey. Keep your antennae up." Jesse stood back and raised his hand in a goodbye salute. As Rachel reached the driveway, she looked through her rear view mirror. Jesse had not moved from where she had left him. She watched as the slump shouldered man moved across the parking lot. Before driving out, she hesitated then leaned against the steering wheel.

Jesse, should I come back to you? Just when I think I'm over you, you come back and turn my world upside down. Is it too late for us?

Return to Leiper's Fork

Chapter 8: The Decision

Jesse woke with a start and jumped to the floor. He was perspiring heavily even in the dark air-conditioned room. As he glanced at the clock he noticed it was three thirty-three in the morning. He thought he'd heard someone scream his name but only the night clerk would know that information. He breathed in deeply as his heart continued pounding. Had he been dreaming? In his mind, he could still hear the voice crying out _ a voice evidently from the bottom of a deep pit. Jesse drew back the drapes.

Everything outside is quiet but I know I heard a woman's voice _ one, I recognize.

He lay back on the cool sheets and closed his eyes. In his mind, he saw a woman standing near the locked gate at the worksite. The sky was dark and the wind was whipping her brown hair. A long dark dress swirled around her feet and she fought to keep a cloak on her shoulders. Each time she tried to stand, the wind knocked her down again. She held up an ancient stained map in one hand. The lower right corner bore the words, Village of Leiper's Fork. From out of nowhere, a man appeared and tried to snatch the map from her hands. She shrieked, and clutched it tighter. Looking into his dark angry face, she screamed again. "Leiper's Fork is mine! You can't have it!"

The man lunged forward and grasped the map from her hands. "I'll give Leiper's Fork to you when you come to me. Until then, I hold it in my hands. You must come when you love me. Only then can it happen." The man whispered hoarsely, as his fingers pointed to the woman who crouched at his feet. His gray eyes angrily pierced hers. "The man you have now has nothing to offer you but pain. If I leave, you will be destroyed."

As the wind blew harder, it eventually sucked in an old mansion that set on a hill nearby. The man, peering at the sky recognized the structure as Steedmore, his ancestral home. After being tossed and whirled by the wind, the twenty six room mansion was hurled to the ground and after a loud crash, a cloud of black dust rose over Leiper's Fork and lingered for some time.

What once was, will be no more.

Hearing a thud, Jesse jumped. He guessed he had fallen back to sleep after the dream. Was the thud caused by a suitcase or vacuum cleaner hitting his door? Sitting up, he tried to make sense of it all. He knew there was a struggle over Leiper's Fork and he knew he loved Rachel. He had even tried to warn her of Carter. He had plans he wanted to accomplish but would she love him after they were completed? He remembered leaving the reunion, the night before and checking into a hotel. He also remembered Rachel's words.

"I'm a Christian and as difficult as it is to live the Christian life, I'm holding out for a Godly man. I'm not going to be unequally yoked to a man who will make my life miserable after the honeymoon. That may sound strange to you Jesse, but it is straight from the heart and I'm waiting for the man who will love me and give me the family I've always wanted. I'm holding out if it takes a lifetime."

Jesse grew angry, remembering her words.

Unequally yoked? What did she mean by that? I've had more money than she'll ever have. I'm a good person. I try to help people and in time, many will know that. She's just being high minded like a lot of Christians. I may not be a Christian but I'm not a fake. I may not be perfect but neither were Mom and Dad and I'm sure they're in Heaven. They were good people too. Never went to church but they were good moral people. Just look what Dad did for the college. That should have got him a lot of brownie points in Heaven.

Jesse groaned. "Rachel, I love you. Always have and always will. Without you by my side, I have nothing and am nothing." He clinched his fists. "I can't remain in Tennessee unless you love me."

How right you are, Jesse. You're a smart man. Just look where you are now. You didn't get here by accident. So far, so good. What was good enough for your parents is good enough for you. Rachel wants too much from you. Forget her.

"No!" Jesse shook his head and whispered into the early morning quiet. "Have I believed a lie all my life? If everything I've believed is true, why

Return to Leiper's Fork

am I so miserable?" In the depths of his heart, Jesse knew the answer to his question. He remembered his dream of Steedmore and the generations that had never darkened the door of any church. They had trusted in their riches but their riches had failed them. Material riches and social status were what they craved and he knew in his heart it wasn't enough for him. One day he would die and everything he possessed would go to another relative or a social cause. Jesse wanted more and at that moment, every wall he had built against God, fell. Jesse stumbled to his knees and cried, "Jesus, help!"

After what seemed like hours, he stood up. The heaviness of a lifetime had lifted and he felt strength he had never felt before. He had wept buckets and in the process of being broken, joy welled up inside him. He had known happiness but never deep abiding joy. He felt like a warrior preparing for battle. It didn't matter how big the giant was, Jesse could defeat him, as David defeated Goliath. David's only artillery had been a smooth stone. Jesse chuckled. He'd heard the story at a church he had visited after Susanna left him. Hadn't David picked up five stones from a brook? He had an arsenal in his leather bag. He'd defeated Goliath with one and had four more stones in reserve for his four brothers, should they appear. Not only did he defeat a giant and an army, but received the king's daughter as his prize.

Father, how I would love to win your daughter for my wife. I have decided to serve you from this day forward. Help me to defeat the enemy and I will give you the praise and glory.

Jesse found himself whistling as he shaved. He had an important meeting in Houston today. After reaching into his suitcase, he unfolded a starched white shirt and pulled his suit from the closet. After tying a perfect knot, he combed his hair and smiled at the handsome man in the mirror. The man smiled back. Breathing a large sigh of relief, he knew he could go into the world of government and do battle. No giant in the oil business could stand in his way, even if that giant guarded gates in Washington, DC. Jesse patted his pocket. He was a warrior now with steel on his hip. Maybe it was only his silver cell phone but it felt like a weapon. He made a mental note to visit a Christian book store. He needed to find out more about the only God to whom he had just committed his life.

Jesse Boy, today your life is taking a turn for the best. I don't care if you have to crawl on your hands and knees. You will do whatever it takes to win Rachel's love. You've already completed the first transaction. You're the son of the King. Wow! If Rachel only knew what happened to you today! The best part is, you didn't do it for her, you did it for yourself.

Jesse hummed as he pushed a button on his phone. He was grateful Betsy had given him the number last year, after Randall's death. He remembered what she had said when he called and asked if he could have it.

As she handed him a slip of paper, Betsy pointed to him with her finger.

"Don't you ever tell Rachel I gave her number to you, Jesse. You've always been my friend and so has she. If this ever develops into something more than friendship, I'd better be the first to know." Jesse sent roses the next day and the local florist wondered why Jesse Steed was sending flowers to a married woman, with an enclosure reading,

A promise is a promise- J.S.

Though his stomach rumbled, breakfast would have to wait. He had better things to do than eat. His heart raced, as he thought of the words he'd say to Rachel. How would she accept his decision? After several rings, he hung up, disappointed. Where could Rachel be so early in the morning? Fear gripped his heart. He knew more than he had told her about Carter but he could be sued if he revealed confidential information. If she was with Carter this early in the morning that meant . . . "Jesse rubbed his jaw and hurried down the hall to the elevator. He couldn't think like that. He knew Rachel or at least thought he did. His problem was with Carter and his conniving ways.

Rachel rushed to the kitchen and grabbed her cell but it was too late. The caller was Jesse. How she wished it had been a telemarketer trying to sell her a vacuum cleaner or someone taking a survey about her smoke detector. Her heart would not have been concerned but this call was different.

Why did he call?

Her eyes fell on the open letter on her counter. The logo was familiar _ Community Bank. Rachel had watched her pennies and made partial monthly payments but surely she wouldn't lose the cabin. Something was better than nothing, wasn't it? "I'll call the bank. Surely they wouldn't take the house when I have tried to do right." In her heart she knew the answer

Return to Leiper's Fork

as she read the last paragraph for the second time.

Due to the amount of your loan, Community Bank must foreclose. From this date forward, Community Bank cannot accept partial payment. We regret this decision but you have (30) THIRTY days to make a full monthly payment or pay the remainder of the loan in full. If you decide otherwise, Community Bank will take possession of your property the first of the next month.

Yours truly,
Mr. Simon Bond
Vice President/Home Mortgage

A call to the bank confirmed the intent of the letter. With a heavy heart, Rachel realized a miracle would have to occur or she would lose her beloved cabin. Borrowing from her parents was not an option. Mr. Locke worked in the lumber mills and it took all he made to put food on the table. Randall's father had been crippled since the accident and his mother still took in ironings to help financially. Rachel looked around the cabin and moaned. Her beloved cabin! How could she give it up? Where would she live? Her parent's house was not an option. Five rooms would not give her room to breathe, much less the privacy she wanted and needed. There would be no place to paint and she could not bring Carter to the Benton's home.

As she thought of her cabin and the man who had built it, Rachel knew Randall's finger prints were everywhere. He had laid each stone in the fireplace and placed each beam across the ceilings. He had laughingly written their initials on top of the last beam and Rachel had kissed him after seeing it.

"One day, when the time is right, we'll show our children the initials. Until then, it will be our secret. When I kiss you under the beam, you'll know why."

As she walked from room to room that evening, she knew why she loved the oak cabin. Overlooking the living room was a stair balustrade of rhododendron branches quite common to cabins built in the early 1900's. Room size hooked rugs, in shades of melon, red, sage and pewter introduced a fresh color palette. Her upholstered pieces were in ivory and melon and one large wall held an antique French cupboard that Rachel filled with blue Willow Ware dishes. The dining room chandelier had been made from reindeer antlers and the fireplace was built from stones they had gathered from the creek. Randall had created large oak cabinets for the kitchen and a pie safe which could have held numerous pies. Rachel's antiques, with their time worn finishes filled each room of her cabin and she was proud of each piece.

Each morning, the golden sun flooded her master bedroom and for their first anniversary, Randall had spent hours creating a king size bentwood bed and later, matching rockers. And the slipper tub in her pink bathroom! How could she leave it? How many nights had she spent soaking in it, after an exhausting day at work?

Rachel's herb garden flourished outside the large screened in porch which featured French doors. She had been delighted when her mother and father brought starts from their garden and used aged manure to encourage them to flourish. Hollyhocks touched the roof at the back and Russian Sage stuck out its long green neck, to catch the first rays of sun. Rosemary, sage, lemon balm, basil, oregano and parsley lifted their heads and sought to romance French Lavender, and Lambs Ear. River stones lined the walk which had been paved with slabs of limestone collected from the nearby cliffs. The warm evenings were now scented with lavender and pineapple geraniums and a jasmine bush which grew near the edge of the porch. Rachel loved it all. This house and everything in it and around it was a gift and it broke her heart to think she would have to leave it.

In the fall, Rachel gathered, tied and hung clusters of lavender to dry. At Christmas, she wrapped the dried foliage with their purple heads in dark tissue, placed them in narrow white boxes and wrapped them with ribbon. At times, she filled beautiful glass jars with the purple heads, placed them in bags and gave them as gifts. Everyone enjoyed her rose potpourri and coveted her home-made treasures. After gathering special plants and grasses, which grew in the fields and along the roadsides, Rachel created huge wreaths with bows of raffia and ribbon and placed them to sell in local businesses. Friends and family knew that Rachel Benton's cabin would always be festive and ready for any holiday. Already, she had placed a large wreath of pink and yellow roses on her door.

She stroked the smooth top of the antique walnut table Randall had refinished. It was then she would have lost it except for the ringing of her cell. Seizing it, she noticed the name, *Jesse Steed*. Quarreling with herself, she wanted to close the cover but her heart overruled her head.

"Rachel, are you crying?"

"Jesse, don't ask silly questions. Why should I be crying? Maybe I have an allergy to ragweed. It is in season you know."

"From what I remember about summers in Tennessee, it's in season but Tennessee women still cry, don't they? Are you feeling bad or did your latest love ditch you?"

"You didn't call to see if I was crying and my love life is my personal business. What do you want?"

"I called to talk." Jesse waited, wondering if Rachel would hang up.

"We don't have anything to say to each other, Jesse. I thought I made it clear when we talked the other night. Where are you anyway?"

Jesse sighed. "I just happen to be in Houston. That's Texas in case you care. Got here and found some lunch at the airport. You know that bag of roasted peanuts and small coke they hand out, don't last long, especially on an empty stomach." He laughed. "I'll only be here a few days. I tried to call you this morning but you either weren't at home or refused to take my call."

Rachel thought for a minute. "I was home. I was on the screened porch reading my mail and before I could get in the door, you hung up."

Relief flooded Jesse.

Rachel was at home and not with Carter. Hallelujah!

"I saw a missed call from you but had no intention of returning it. Was there something important you needed to tell me? I am expecting Carter later and I need to freshen up a bit before he arrives." Rachel spoke pointedly, hoping he would hang up.

At the mention of the name, Carter, Jesse's heart plummeted. "No,

Rachel. I did have something I wanted to tell you but maybe I shouldn't have called. Just wondered how you were doing. You know, we can still be friends, even though you're tied up with that artist. I won't keep you however. I'm on my way to DC on business and I wanted to hear your sweet southern voice. It's always soothing, even if you do jab me at times with your silver pointed tongue." She heard Jesse exhale. "Get your little face ready for Carter, honey. We wouldn't want that perfectionist to be disappointed, would we?"

Rachel closed her cell before she realized what she had done. "He makes me so angry! Jesse Steed is the most selfish, arrogant man I know. I am glad he lost every dime he had. If he thinks he can come and go and twist Rachel Lea Benton around his little finger, he has another thing coming. He wouldn't know the word, goodbye, if it smacked him in his handsome face. For now, I'd better put on my makeup or Carter is going to tell me he's not too happy with the way I look."

Why in the world is Jesse going to Washington, DC?

Chapter 9: Engaged

Carter and Rachel sat in the living room of the cabin as the evening sunlight filtered through the windows. "Carter, before I accept this ring, I need to know if you really love me. Am I the woman you want for the rest of your life?" Rachel carefully studied the man, who sat beside her. Was there a flicker of surprise in his eyes? For the first time, she noticed patches of gray at his temples and soft crinkles around his eyes. He looked older than he had before he left. How had furrows filled his brow in one week? As she met his eyes, a muscle twitched at the corner of his jaw. Did it matter that he was older? Would it matter in a few years when he was fifty? What about sixty? Did age matter, if a couple loved each other?

Carter embraced her. "Well darling, of course you are the woman I want for the rest of my life. I would be crazy if I thought otherwise. If your mind is whirling about the woman I told you about, don't let that bother you. There's no need to go there again. It's been over for a long time. She was never wife material as far as I was concerned. It's true, she didn't want to end our relationship but it was time, and I was ready. Let's put it in the past." He cupped her chin and looked in her eyes. "I've missed you, my sweet. Missed you so much I could hardly stay away. Let me slip this diamond on your finger and tell the world how much you mean to me."

Rachel put up her hand, as if protecting her heart. "Carter, when Randall died, I promised myself I would never marry a man who was not a Christian. What you think about God is very important to me."

With eyes narrowing and nostrils flaring, Carter shot her a glance. His words exploded from his mouth like a cannon ball out of a cannon.

"Rachel, who is God? What is God? Is there a God? Do you want me to play the game of twenty questions?" Not waiting for an answer, he continued. "Let me propose a question to you. What if we are gods?" After seeing her shocked expression, he laughed. "Can't you just be happy, that I've asked you to marry me and be done with it? What is all this religious stuff? I've never bothered with it before and until I see a need for God, whoever, whatever, he is, I won't bother with it." Carter was frustrated at the woman dressed in lavender capris and a white sleeveless top. He studied her a moment, noting how every detail about her was perfect. "Listen honey, I've been gone all week, and I brought you this ring. I want you to be my wife. Can we stop the serious talk and plan our lives? I'm here to talk about marriage. I've waited two years, for this day. I want a wife and a home. I love you and I love my job." He reached over to kiss her, but Rachel turned away. She had seen Carter in a different light and her world was shaken.

She pressed further, ignoring his annoyed look. "You never mentioned children. Would you like to be a father, Carter? You know I'm not getting any younger. I'll be thirty, one day and if we marry, I'd like to have a baby right away. I don't want to wait until I'm in a wheelchair and am too feeble to hold my child." At his look of disbelief, Rachel giggled. "Sarah had a baby when she was ninety years old."

"Who? What?" Her words stunned Carter. "You know a woman who had a baby at ninety? That is an absolute impossibility. Are you trying to make me into a fool, Rachel?

"She lived a long, long time ago, Carter _ in Bible days. Didn't you ever hear the story about Abraham and Sarah? Remember when the angel came and told her she was going to have a baby and she laughed? That's what Isaac means, laughter."

"Who is Isaac, Rachel? I have no idea who you are talking about. You talk about an old woman getting pregnant when I'm trying to convince you to marry me." Carter grimaced and reached for his glass of tea. He swallowed long, hoping Rachel would give up her religious stories. All of that was fantasy to him. In time, he would convince her of the same.

"Carter, I don't want to bore you but that was a true story. If you've got a Bible you can read it yourself." A moment of silence followed, as Carter pretended to study the ceiling and twiddle his thumbs.

"Can we dismiss our study of religion and let me slip this ring on your finger?" We've got a lifetime to talk about God. Please give me your attention, lovely creature and kiss me after I slip this exquisite ring on your finger. It cost me a fortune, so I hope you'll appreciate all I've done. I sold

Return to Leiper's Fork

my house in Little Rock and your ring darn near cost me what I got out of the deal, especially when I had to pay the closing costs for the couple whose realtor was a total shark."

Rachel's eyes lit up when she saw the large stone. "Carter! You shouldn't have bought such an expensive ring. I would never expect you to spend so much money on me. Oh, it is so beautiful! Look at it sparkle!" As Carter held the pear shaped diamond to the light, the ceiling flooded with thousands of tiny shimmers. Slowly, he slid the ring on her finger. "Miss Benton, will you marry me? I'll make you the happiest woman in Leiper's Fork."

He cupped her chin and kissed her, as she whispered, "I will." Afterward, she shuddered, and her eyes filled with tears.

Carter drew back and was thrilled he'd brought the ring with him. "I know they're tears of happiness, darling. I'm glad you love me so much." Carter smiled, as he tenderly wiped her eyes. Now he knew she truly loved him. The ring had definitely won her over, religious convictions or none. Carter knew he could buy her if the prize was big enough. That night, Rachel had difficulty sleeping but it had nothing to do with her engagement to Dr. Carter Viking.

In his hotel room that evening, Jesse quickly thumbed through the pages of a book he had purchased in the bookstore. He had finally chosen one which promised he could learn the Bible in twenty-four hours. Twenty-four hours! He didn't think he could stay awake that long but he was hungry. Hungry to learn as much as he could and if he didn't finish, he would read it on the plane. His stomach growled. Calling down to the desk, he asked the clerk if she knew of a great place for dinner.

In her Texas drawl, the evening clerk responded, "Yes, sir, I do. When you come down, I'll have directions printed on a piece of paper. The prices are right and the food is excellent. You won't be disappointed."

Jesse mumbled to himself, as he drove, "Turn left out of the hotel, go down over the railroad tracks and make a right over the highway. Go about two miles and turn into that little town. It should be on the left, right across from the large Methodist Church. She said I can't miss it."

Immediately, he spied the large white house setting on a corner, having a winding gray porch. Long green shutters bordered the windows and six tall columns stood at attention, welcoming the tired guest. The day was hot and Jesse was hungry. The smells of food in the evening air made his stomach rumble. He smiled at the cheerful wreath of yellow and pink flowers. He knew someone who had a similar one on her cabin door.

Suddenly, the door opened and Jesse was ushered into a large foyer.
"Good evening, sir. Welcome to Swanson House. I'll be glad to seat you in the red room unless you'd prefer to sit elsewhere." After seating him, the tall thin waiter with thick glossy hair and thin moustache promised he would bring iced water and fresh hot rolls with butter. "The rolls are compliments of the house. In fact, they are very popular with our diners."

After placing his order, Jesse looked around. The large cherry red room had four windows that welcomed the last rays of the evening sun. The fireplace had been painted a glossy white to match the trim in the room and it reminded Jesse of a red velvet cake with white icing. To complete the warm décor, a large painting of red poppies had been placed over the fireplace and the adjacent wall held a water color of Swanson House.

When the waiter returned, Jesse questioned him about the building.
"Well, sir, this building was originally a livery stable in 1790. During the next century, a large hall and a few rooms were added and in the 1930's a kindergarten was established here. The first mayor lived here for some time. If you'd like, visit the yellow room after you finish dinner and look at the south window. You'll see initials scratched in one of the panes. They've been there for eighty-four years."

Jesse interrupted. "Who was the famous person?"

"Sir, I'm going to get to that in just a second. That's where the story gets interesting. It seems that Miss Noreen, the kindergarten teacher questioned a young man and his fiancé who visited her school. Being an inquisitive teacher, she wanted to know if the stone in the woman's ring was a genuine diamond or a piece of glass. 'Is that diamond real or is it glass?' The teacher stepped back, assuming the stone had cost only a few dollars. The man's fiancé stood nervously blushing. What would either say if the stone was glass? Would the man use the Depression as an excuse? The smiling young man proudly slipped the ring from his fiancés finger and slowly touched it

Return to Leiper's Fork

to the cold pane of glass. Two sets of eyes were on him, as he deftly scratched their initials. To the teacher's surprise and certainly the future bride's, the letters, SW + ES were etched in glass. The man had purchased a genuine diamond ring and he stood back smiling broadly, as his future bride looked relieved and moved toward his embrace. That day, the proof was not in the pudding but definitely in the pane of glass."

Jesse's eyes blinked quickly. He too, had been in love with a young woman, years ago. He had even purchased a diamond ring and was ready to pop the question. Even though he was young, he knew he wanted to marry Rachel Locke before they started college. Prom night was the night he had chosen to surprise her. He had won a scholarship to San Francisco state and he wanted to take the girl of his dreams with him as his wife. They'd had a silly argument and he'd stalked off in anger. He'd not spoken to her in two weeks. She, in her pride and stubbornness refused to accept his call.

He'd seen her walking toward her car with Randall Benton, but Randall had nothing to offer her. He never dated girls in high school. Sure, he was a basketball star but Rachel wouldn't get serious about him. Randall Benton was no competition to any senior guy. If Rachel was still hurt, she deserved it. Even though she was beautiful, talented and stubborn, Jesse loved her. He hurried over to her car and found Randall kissing her cheek.

After swallowing his pride, he asked for the color of her dress. Prom was only a few days away. At first, he thought she was bluffing about going with Randall but when he went to her house that night, she refused to come down from her bedroom. When he heard she was going with Randall, Jesse scrambled to ask Susanna Southhall, all the while hating himself for doing so.

He and Susanna arrived to find Randall holding Rachel on the dance floor. Her head was on his shoulder and the situation looked cozier than Jesse thought it should. She refused to dance with him, after he tapped Randall on the back. That night, Jesse walked out of her life forever. Prom night had been ruined for him and he had taken Susanna home early. As the lovely Susanna, dressed in black satin, lifted her lips to his, Jesse had turned aside. He saw Rachel's face as Susanna moved closer. He wanted nothing more than to follow Randall and send him and his dented green truck over an embankment. He wiped his brow not believing how jealousy could lead to destruction. His mind argued that if Rachel loved him, she'd make up but summer passed and Rachel went on with her life.

Before he left for San Francisco, Jesse sadly returned the engagement ring to the jeweler's. Both he and Rachel had gone their own way and he had not seen her until his parents were killed. By then he was a senior in college with a promising career. All of his time and energy had been spent preparing for his future. One day he'd return to Leiper's Fork, a wealthy man. Rachel would be sorry, she had snubbed him. Maybe then she'd return and ask his forgiveness. After his parent's accident, he'd gone for a walk in the woods. He needed to get away _ to grieve, alone. He'd heard a car coming up the driveway but never thought it would be Rachel Benton. He'd almost stumbled on the driveway, when he realized what a beautiful woman she had become. No longer was she the thin high school senior. That day she was a woman and more desirable than Jesse could believe.

As he approached the house, he found her standing on the driveway with her arms full of paper plates and cutlery. In his grief, he'd wanted to run to her and bury his face against her softness but he knew he could not. He ached to be with the only girl he'd ever loved but he was hurt knowing she was in love with Randall. He'd heard all of the gossip from Betsy. Randall and Rachel would be married in weeks. His future with Rachel was over but it was difficult to accept. He'd bowed out long ago but never given up hope. He only wanted Rachel's happiness, even though the thought of her with Randall hurt him deeply. Why was it so difficult for him to get over his first love? Rachel Locke would never wear his ring and he would never see her become his bride. Later, he had graduated. Opportunities to travel the world were opened to him and through hard work and wise investments he had acquired a fortune. In time, mostly due to loneliness, he married the lovely Susanna, who refused to leave him alone. They took a vacation to Europe for their honeymoon and Jesse hoped with all his heart, he would forget Rachel but his effort was fruitless. After a year, Susanna filed for divorce.

One day, Betsy called to tell Jesse, Randall had died and it caught Jesse off guard. He was sorry that Randall had suffered _ maybe more sorry for all the bad thoughts he'd had against the popular basketball coach. But had fate intervened? Could he win Rachel's love again? He knew he could never rush her. He'd seen Rachel across the wave of mourners the day of the funeral.! There she was, less than twelve feet in front of him, dressed in a black summer dress. He could tell her heart was broken as her brown eyes filled with tears again and again. How Jesse wanted to dry them and hold

Return to Leiper's Fork

her until her sorrow ended. She'd lost weight and he saw she was only a shadow of the woman he had seen six years before. But there she stood, still beautiful in his eyes. He watched as she bit her lip and pushed back a wayward lock of golden brown hair. He'd wanted to talk with her but after he softly touched her arm, she'd screamed and run away. Jesse left town after apologizing. His dream for Leiper's Fork would be delayed but only out of respect for Rachel's grief.

When he'd heard she lost her teaching position at the high school, he agreed to be on the Board of Trustees. He was following in his father's footsteps but he had a deeper reason than that. He knew his money was behind the college's invitation but he would have given it regardless. As a condition of his acceptance, he'd ask for Rachel Benton to be granted a position in the art department. She had the qualifications and experience needed and if he had to contribute a larger amount of money to ensure her employment, he would. Money had little meaning to him, now. There were greater things to accomplish than create more wealth.

Later, he had battled several of the trustees over the hiring of Dr. Carter Viking but Jesse had been outvoted, even when information about the professor raised many questions. Now, the woman he loved was going to marry the man he had so fervently opposed. With his brown eyes, thick brown hair, thin moustache and spontaneous smile, Carter was a woman's man. Jesse understood how the professor had captured Rachel's heart. He prayed for wisdom and a second chance with her. The God he trusted could slay giants with a stone. If He did it once, He might just do it again.

Rachel. Don't be so strong willed and independent you'll do something you regret. You don't know Carter Viking as I do. If you did, you'd run to get away from him but at this time I can't tell you what I know.

He was jarred from remembering as the waiter set before him a mouthwatering plate of food. Jesse stared at it before glancing up at the waiter. "That was a fascinating story you told me earlier. I'll have to remember it."

The Swanson Restaurant certainly knew how to feed a hungry man and he was ravenous. Before him were three pieces of golden fried chicken, field peas, fried okra and sweet potato soufflé. A basket of homemade rolls and a large glass of iced tea set next to his plate. The waiter appeared briefly. "Now, don't disappoint our pastry chef. She has chess and pecan pie, bread pudding with caramel sauce and chocolate decadence. If you can't eat it here, please take some with you. You might want it before you retire for the night."

After paying his bill, Jesse walked into the large yellow room filled with diners. Each window was attractively decorated with heavy cream drapes featuring ruby accents and a large matching swag trimmed with deep cream fringe. Walking to the north window, Jesse spied the initials on an upper pane. Sure enough, the story was true. He touched the scrawls in the glass. From behind him, a woman spoke. "Is there anything I can do for you, sir?" Jesse looked around, to find an attractive young waitress smiling at him.

"Oh, no! I've already dined and need to pay my bill. The waiter told me the story about the initials on the window and I had to see them myself. Quite a story!" Jesse groaned inwardly as he strode down the walk to his rented car. It seems a birthday party was going to be held in one corner of the porch. Large helium balloons were dancing in the evening breeze and before he got to his car, a long, black limo pulled up beside the restaurant. Children and adults spilled out laughing and yelling. The happy occasion made Jesse feel lonelier than he had ever felt. He laughed harshly. He'd lost the only woman he'd ever wanted to marry and had married and divorced a woman he never loved.

You're a loser, Jesse. A real loser!

Return to Leiper's Fork

Chapter 10: The Exhibit

Jesse stood in shock. Had Bud just told him Rachel was engaged to Carter Viking?

"I know you always carried a torch for Rachel, so I'm sorry I have to break the news to you. I didn't think you should find out by hearing it from anyone else." Bud Bond waited for a response. "Jesse, are you still on the line?"

"What did you just tell me Bud, because I don't think I heard you correctly?" Jesse shook his head in surprise. He had just returned from Houston the night before and had been exhausted all morning. "Do you know when she's marrying him?"

"There wasn't a specific date. The Tennessean reported it would be in the near future. I know she's been under a lot of pressure lately, but I also know Rachel. I've known that girl since elementary school. She's not happy, Jesse. It doesn't take a rocket scientist to figure that out. Last night, I saw her at The Country Store and I had to snap my fingers in front of her face twice to get her attention. She jumped, as if she'd been bitten by a rattlesnake. When I congratulated her, I thought for sure, she was going to get all teary eyed but she held herself pretty well. Just gave me a big hug and held on, like she was getting ready to take a maiden voyage on the Titanic. I don't know anything about that man she's marrying but I've seen worse pictures. He's some art professor at the college and not too bad looking. She could have done worse. She could have married you." Bud snickered but only for a second.

Jesse clinched his jaw and held his cell so tight he thought it would crack. His site manager continued. "Now, for the biggest news to hit The Fork. Hold on to your hat. I don't think this was to get out but somebody told. In fact, it's raced like wild fire. Rachel lost her cabin."

"Wait, partner! What did you say?" A stunned Jesse shook his head in disbelief.

"Jesse, it seems she had some trouble coming up with the money. You know, a lot of people are losing their homes now days. "

"What do you mean Bud? I thought she was doing okay after Randall's death. I mean, she had her art in The Gallery and she worked at the college three nights a week. Not a great situation but I've seen worse." Jesse squeezed his eyes shut for a moment and rested his head against the wall. Was he to intervene in some way or was this something he needed to avoid, regardless of how much it bothered him? "Bud, I'm not a harsh man but I have my limits. Rachel has made her bed and I guess she'll have to lie in it. I thought we had a chance once but that never happened. She is as stubborn as a Missouri mule, so if she's decided to marry Carter, he can take care of her, if he knows how." Jesse sighed. The weight of the world had fallen on his shoulders. "Listen, buddy, I appreciate you calling me. At least I know and when it happens, I won't be totally caught off guard. I've got to get back to work. Maybe I can take you to dinner the next time I'm in Leiper's Fork. Puckett's or Joe Natural's will have to do, unless you want me to eat your wife's cooking."

The college had granted Rachel a leave of absence so she could paint for the exhibit. She was grateful to Carter for speaking in her behalf. If it had not been for him, she couldn't have accepted the offer. She felt honored that her artwork would be featured in a special exhibit at the Frist Center for Visual Arts in Nashville.

"Rachel, you won't be able to paint if you don't take time to do it. You'll be painting day and night and I want it to be your best. Besides, I told the president it would be a plume in the college's hat for all the attention given to one of their staff. He granted you time off with pay, after I stood up for you. Of course, I could have been part of the exhibit but I'd rather see you get the attention and exposure. All I expect to get out of it, is to spend time with my fiancé." Carter smiled and wiped his lips with one of the extra napkins that accompanied the pizza and salad he had brought for dinner.

After critiquing her art, Carter suggested several minor changes. He advised Rachel to use warmer colors which irritated her. She was not upset about being given advice from such a knowledgeable and well known artist but she had her own technique and wanted to use colors that spoke to her.

Return to Leiper's Fork

After watching Rachel paint most of the afternoon, Carter decided to leave. He was bored but knew she needed to work. Rachel was deep in thought, as he kissed her neck and slowly wound his arms around her waist before pulling her against him.

Caught off guard, she jumped at his touch. "Carter! I hope I didn't get any paint on you. I am so sorry. I was so lost in thought about which color to paint the soldier's eyes I didn't realize you were behind me. Forgive me."

Holding her close, he whispered, "Forget it, precious. I wish I was the brush you're holding or the canvas you're painting, because what little attention I've got lately, I think you love them more than me. I am a jealous man, my little artist. If I wasn't expecting a phone call in the next hour, I would stand here and hold you while you paint but I wonder if it would do any good." Hearing no comment he continued. "I'll call you tomorrow and don't forget to set the date for our wedding. I'm getting a bit impatient." He winked at the speechless woman, reminded her to wash the paint out of her hair and sauntered out the door. Rachel laid her brush on the palette. She would only rest for a few minutes. Her day had started before the sun came up and she was already drained.

Only one more day and I'll be ready for the exhibit. Jesse, I'm ashamed to say I need you. I am so sorry you loved me and I threw it all away. I regret what I have done. I've never deserved you.

By the next afternoon, workers had come and each piece of art had been carefully boxed and crated, ready to be taken to the Frist Center and put on display. Her photo would be placed on a pedestal in front of the exhibit and her business cards were already in her purse. Each piece of art had been priced for sale and Rachel hoped each would sell quickly. She had only a little time before the bank would foreclose, and she would have to marry Carter in order to keep her home. The embarrassment of foreclosure would be far more devastating than she could bear. In time she might learn to really love him.

Jesse had spent a lot of time praying. When he thought he knew what to do, he'd change his mind. His instinct told him to go to Nashville. He wanted to see the exhibit and hoped to see Rachel, if only from a distance. Restlessly, he had paced the floor of his office. Finally, he ordered a plane ticket and hastily packed for the early morning flight. He would rent a car and stay in a hotel downtown near the center. Hopefully, he wouldn't see anyone he knew. He had no desire to explain why he had flown thousands of miles to be at Rachel's exhibit when she was engaged to another man. To see her would be painful but to not see her again, would be devastating. Jesse planned to fly back to Seattle, Sunday evening and no one would ever know, he had been in, The Volunteer State.

That Saturday evening, Carter patted Rachel's shoulder, as she stood nervously waiting in the exhibit hall. "Darling, you look so beautiful. My only fear is that someone will want to purchase you. You're a work of art tonight. Simply a masterpiece!" He studied the woman whose golden brown tresses had been styled by a top stylist in Nashville. Evidently, a few hours at the spa, at Carter's expense had transformed a tired woman into an exquisite goddess. A makeup artist had completed Carter's masterpiece, and he knew he had found the woman of his dreams. "That beauty treatment at the spa transformed you, Rachel. You were beginning to look much like a caterpillar. However, I have made you into a beautiful exotic butterfly. You're more gorgeous than I ever realized, even though you should have worn that taupe Dior, I picked out for you. You would have looked ravishing with one shoulder bare. Beauty sells art you know and think of the money you can bring in, if you . . ."

"Carter, I know I've not looked like a raving beauty each time you've seen me but honestly, I've had to get a lot of work done in a very short time. Working women don't have time to powder their nose every five minutes, much less refresh their lipstick. Besides, bare shoulders aren't my style. I'm sorry I reminded you of a caterpillar." Rachel realized it didn't take much for Carter to make her feel inferior. At times, his words cut like knives.

I hope, after we're married, he doesn't expect me to serve breakfast in heels and a silk dress. That man is going to be very disappointed, because Rachel is Rachel and what he sees is what he gets. I'm going to be me until the day I die and I'm never leaving Leiper's Fork. Never!

Carter touched the gold strap of her dress. He smiled admiringly and continued trailing his finger toward her porcelain chin. He liked what the spa had done for her. Even tonight, she would pass for a woman in her early twenties and he was a lover of youth and beauty. "You should try a darker mascara more often. It makes your brown eyes appear larger. I like

Return to Leiper's Fork

everything they did to you at the spy." He trailed kisses up her neck. "That perfume is lovely. Absolutely intoxicating! Every dollar I spent was well worth it, darling. Mona Lisa in all of her glory could never compare to the future Mrs. Carter Viking."

Rachel smiled but her heart was troubled. Today was the day every artist dreamed of and yet she wanted to flee. She felt uncomfortable with Carter and even tried to persuade him not to attend. He had not only come but had made her a previous appointment at the Nashville Spa for a message, makeup session and all the trimmings. What he had spent would pay her utilities for six months. Not only had she heard him tell the dealers and collectors she was his fiancé, but they were invited to attend their wedding at the Opryland Hotel. Never had a peacock strutted so proudly, as Carter Viking as he discussed his wedding. Rachel listened to his conversations, as people viewed her art. "I'm sure sometime in December. Yes, early December. Of course, you are invited. Think nothing of it. We'll be glad to have you." How many had he invited? Rachel turned away not only in disappointment but disgust. She wanted a wedding. Carter wanted a show.

After deliberately avoiding the pre-exhibit festivities, with uniformed waiters and more wine and champagne than any dealer or collector needed or wanted, Jesse quietly visited the lower exhibits. Twenty-four thousand square feet of gallery space had been donated to the visual arts. Everywhere Jesse looked were works of photography, oil sketches, water colors, topographical landscapes hoping to decry the human scarring of the land, and the most beautiful quilts he had ever seen. Local, state and regional artists across Tennessee had their works on display and hundreds of dealers and collectors were there to snap up treasures.

When Jesse saw someone he knew, he quickly avoided them. He knew Rachel's paintings were on the top floor of what had once been the Nashville post office. He watched from a distance as admirers and buyers crowded around her. He remembered the gold dress she wore at the reunion. It had fit her like a glove but had she lost weight? Even though she looked gorgeous, she somehow seemed weary. How he wanted to hold and protect her. Wasn't that what he had read in his latest book _ that men should see women as a beautiful vessel to protect?

As he watched across the wave of people, he saw Carter's arm wrap possessively around Rachel's waist and she seemed annoyed at his public display of affection. Standing near a column, Jesse mumbled below his breath. "Carter, you've won the only woman I've ever loved and you'd better take good care of her or I'll come after you and you won't be smiling when I finish with you."

Rachel was never one for public display. She would hardly allow me to hug her in public even at the football game after we dated four months. Somehow, I always admired her for that, even if I didn't like it at the time. Rachel Benton is a lady and a modest one at that.

A large canvas caught his eye as he started to turn in the direction of the escalator. *The Promise!* He had seen it at the cabin. Why was Rachel selling a painting that meant so much to her?

I guess she is financially desperate. Did she lose her house? I'm not too sure what to do now but my Father knows. I'll ask him for wisdom.

His heart raced within him.

I can't take the painting to Seattle with me but it could be placed in a storage facility until it's needed.

He placed a call to a friend. He knew what he had to do and he didn't have time to spare. Already, several people were crowded around the painting and one woman was trying to talk her husband into purchasing it.

In the distance, a young woman in pink plucked the gold strings of a large harp and violinists played melodies in other wings of the exhibit. Waiters passed with tiny sandwiches, small pastries, caviar, and tall fluted glasses filled to the brim with champagne costing $200.00 a bottle.

As Carter handed a glass to Rachel, she shook her head and smiled.
"No, Carter. I don't drink. I'm sorry but thanks. You are very thoughtful." After swirling the glass several times, Carter decided to drain it. The pear flavor, aromas of rose and toasted nut made it a perfect selection for the evening function. As he set his glass on a tray, Carter wondered how he could change his future bride. So far, they had nothing in common but a love for art.

As Jesse drank in the sight of the smiling woman with flushed face and

Return to Leiper's Fork

pink lips, he knew he had never seen her so lovely. She was beautiful indeed but this woman at the exhibit was not his Rachel. The Rachel he knew, needed little makeup. She was wholesome and the clean country air at Leiper's Fork kept a glow on her face and a blush on her cheeks that no expensive makeup could ever do. His Rachel didn't need a designer dress. She was a princess in faded jeans and a tee shirt and that suited him just fine. As Jesse turned to descend the escalator, he watched Carter kiss Rachel. Evidently, the professor had been served too many times. Jesse was disturbed.

Probably the last time I will see her in my life and I have to leave her with Carter.

As Rachel opened her eyes and stared at the crowd, she met a set of steel gray eyes staring at her. Her pink lips opened slowly in surprise, as her flushed face paled. She mouthed his name and watched as Jesse left the room.

Immediately after Jesse arrived at the bottom floor, he entered the cashier's office. "I need to make a confidential transaction. I'd prefer the artist not know who purchased her painting." A few seconds later, he handed a check to the cashier, while repeating his warning. "Remember to keep this confidential. I'd hate to see what would happen if the artist finds out who purchased it. Send the painting to this address on Monday and make sure there is no damage to the canvas." He handed the slip of paper to the man whose hands trembled.

The cashier adjusted his glasses and swept back strands of graying hair.
"Sir, this check exceeds the sale price of the painting. I mean, you have made a huge mistake in the amount."

Gray eyes matched green ones. "No mistake at all, sir. The extra beyond the cost, is to be given to the artist as a gift and I will find out if she receives it. I hope there is no misunderstanding about this."

"Point perfectly made, sir. It was good to do business with you. The painting will be crated and shipped to the address you gave me. Thank you for your purchase and have a wonderful day, uh, Mr. Steed." The cashier stroked his moustache and turned to place the check in his drawer. He had heard of strange things in his life but he had never heard of tipping an artist thousands of dollars.

Rachel's conversation with Tony Hunter ended sooner than she wished but she needed to get back to her exhibit. "Carter! Did you hear what that gentleman asked me to do? I can't believe, he wants me to paint murals for a museum in Leiper's Fork. So that is what they are building. A fine secret they have kept! Everyone assumed it was some type of great house with all those drives and landscaping. Some said a barn but no one knew for sure what JHR Corporation was building. They've sure been mum. Anyway, he asked if he could meet me Monday and work out a few details."

Carter's eyes slid away from hers. "Rachel, having a special showing of your work is important but painting murals for a museum in Leiper's Fork is nothing to brag about. You're not at the top, my dear. Don't let all of this attention go to your head. I've been there and I'm still humble. Quit orbiting and return to earth, darling."

Rachel placed her hands on her hips and whispered harshly, "Carter Viking! I think I've been very earthbound all my life. I may never be a Monet or Picasso but I have truly been blessed to have my work on exhibit at the Frist Center. You wouldn't be jealous would . . . ?" In frustration, she hissed, "Forget it, Carter. I should not have gone there. I'm just physically and emotionally worn out."

Carter regretted his remarks, but only momentarily. "You know honey, I'm tired too. What do you say I take you home and we eat out another night? I've got some work to do before tomorrow. I spent the day with you and got nothing accomplished for myself."

Rachel was ashamed of herself after all he had done for her and how she had treated him. "Carter, you were great to talk to the dealers, collectors and everyone else who showed. I will have to cook dinner for you one night. You name it and I'll have you a banquet meal. Steak? Chicken? Shrimp?" Rachel offered a peck to his cheek.

Indignation showed on his face. "To think, that is all I get for everything I've done. A peck on the cheek! Honey, you sure are stingy with your gratitude but maybe you'll warm up some day. See you Monday night after class and I do expect to see you." With a wave of his hand, he left. Rachel would have to drive herself home.

Return to Leiper's Fork

After church on Sunday, Rachel organized her studio and cleaned house most of the afternoon. "Drat you cobwebs and dust. You're going to disappear because Miss Rachel is coming after you with her dust cloth and vacuum cleaner." After hitting and missing in her cabin for weeks on end, Rachel decided she'd had enough of a dirty house. She'd noticed Carter staring at the jars of brushes and dirty dishes in the sink, when he picked her up Saturday. She laughed at the thought of a dust bunny in Carter's apartment. He was too impeccable for his own good. She had never seen a hair out of place or a wrinkle in his clothing. How could they ever live together, when they were both so opposite? At the end of the evening, the cabin glowed and smelled as fresh as the day it was built.

After resting for a few moments, Rachel pulled the exhibit check from her purse. She had looked at it the night before, and was so surprised, she could hardly sleep. In church that morning, she had written out a fat check and placed it in the offering. "God, you are so good to me." She squealed, and danced happily around the room. "This check will pay more than half my loan to the bank. Tomorrow, if I agree to paint the murals, I'll ask for an advance. Surely, a major corporation like JHR, can advance little ole me a big fat check. At least it won't hurt to ask."

She hummed busily, until evening shadows filled the cabin. Another beautiful Tennessee day would soon disappear and she welcomed the dark of night. The large oak cabin, on the rural lane took on a beauty of its own, as lamplight spilled out into the velvety darkness. Rachel drooled, as she pulled a small cobbler from the oven. As soon as her mitten touched the baking dish, she heard a knock at her door. "Just a minute! I've got my hands full. Carter is that you?"

Chapter 11: Dinner for Two

The caller waited a few moments, then slowly opened Rachel's door. He held a large bouquet of red roses in his hand. "Rachel, sorry to disappoint you but it's not Carter. Do I smell cobbler? Maybe, cherry or blackberry?"

"Jesse!" Rachel yelped, as she stumbled to the counter. Dark hot juice spilled on her mitt. "Ouch! My mitt must have had a hole in it. I've burned myself." Rachel grimaced and sucked her finger.

Jesse set the bouquet down quickly and hurried to her side. "Allow me to help. Remember, I was a Boy Scout years ago. Let me hold your hand under some cold water. If that doesn't work they can take away one of my medals." They both laughed, as Jesse gently held Rachel's soft one in his. As they stood close, he smelled the sweet scent of her hair and she smelled his classic clean cologne. Her hand felt small and soft in his large one and he relished the moment. It felt right and good to be with Rachel again. It had been far too long, since he had been this close to her.

She took the flowers and opened the cabinet for a vase. "You know the earth laughs with all of its flowers." Choosing a large one, she filled the vase with water and inserted the roses. "I'll cut the stems later. Jesse, why did you come? I mean, last night. You do know that Carter and I . . ."

"Why did I come? I probably smelled that cobbler down the road. You do know that blackberry is my favorite, don't you? And as for Carter, the whole world knows you two are engaged. That's old news by now. I'm not jealous. Don't worry." He smiled and reached for a spoon and bowl.

"Jesse Steed! I didn't ask why you came to my house. I want to know why you came to the exhibit yesterday. You don't live in Tennessee anymore. By the way, did you ask if you could have some cobbler?" Not waiting for a reply, she looked at the man who had taken off his jacket and was rolling up his sleeves. "Did you hear me? I asked why you came to the exhibit at the Fist Center, last night."

Return to Leiper's Fork

Jesse turned with a half grin. "Rachel. I never work on an empty stomach." He patted his flat midriff then reached into the refrigerator to get a glass of milk. "I see you have hamburger patties already made up. Would you happen to have a few potatoes in your bin? I've been thinking about French fries and homemade burgers all day." He reached in the pantry for a skillet and got out salt and pepper. "A slice of onion, and a few dill pickles and mustard might help those burgers. They usually do you know. I can't believe I'm getting a home cooked meal for once. That on the road food, gets mighty tiresome after a while." Ignoring her, he continued. "Did you ever read the book entitled, *Stone Soup*, where the soldier was hungry and tricked the town folk into giving him all the ingredients he needed to make soup? He only had a stone. Imagine that! He must have been one smart fellow." He looked around at the baffled woman. "I'm supposing you've got an apron somewhere in this fine kitchen. I'd hate to get grease on my new shirt."

Rachel smiled, as she reached for her most feminine apron. She especially liked the pink one trimmed with lace. Before Jesse could say, "Catsup!" she had it tied in a large bow at his back. When she finished, he looked at her and grunted, "I'm sure you didn't have one for a male." Rachel laughed. She could outwit this handsome man in seconds.

"Now, Mr. Steed, you look like you belong in a kitchen. I'm only helping you look the part but if you ever want to be domesticated, you can have your wife purchase you an apron that's not so frilly." Seeing smoke rise from her stove, she shrieked, "Don't burn my skillet!"

"Aye! Aye! Miss Benton." Jesse tweaked her cheek, after moving the skillet and pitching the flaming dishtowel in the sink. "Guess, I owe you a new dishtowel, huh?" He then searched for plates and utensils while Rachel threw the burned towel in the trash and shook her head. In minutes, the fries were golden brown and the burgers were placed on warm crusty buns. Jesse's mouth watered but the food wasn't as tantalizing as the woman sitting near him. He cleared his throat. "I always start my meals with prayer Miss Benton, so I'll have to ask you to drop that fry, until I pray."

Rachel not only dropped her fry but her mouth as Jesse bent his dark head and gave thanks for their meal. Never in a hundred years did she ever think she would hear him pray before a meal or at any other occasion. A miracle surely had happened! Afterward, Jesse calmly shook his napkin, laid it in his lap and speared a fry before looking up at the woman, who was still staring at him.

"Eat up, Rachel. I didn't shave my handsome face to have you stare at it." Jesse pointed at her with his fork to make his point, then quickly speared another golden fry and smothered it with catsup. Rachel blushed from head to toe. She had only meant to look at the man at her table for a few minutes but he had caught her. He still had that funny little cowlick in the front of his hair and the dimple in his chin. She loved the way his dark hair curled on his collar. What a handsome dinner companion. As she thought of how she missed being with him, Rachel's heart beat out of control. Her mind was screaming this couldn't be happening. Jesse was in her kitchen sharing a meal and she knew she should ask him to leave . . . but she couldn't.

We're just friends. That's all there is to it. I'm getting married soon. Can't friends enjoy a last meal together? Sure! Judas had a last meal with Jesus and ending up betraying him.

Her mind argued with her heart but her heart won the battle. "Jesse, why did you come back to Nashville? I saw you Saturday at the Frist Center, didn't I?" Rachel gave him a searching look but he turned away. "Jesse. It doesn't really matter. You can come and go when you like but I hope you don't get fired. A lot of people need jobs now days and working at a filling station is nothing to sneeze at. And now I must talk to you about these." She pointed to the splashes of red in the tall glass vase. "Jesse, those roses are too expensive. You really shouldn't have."

"You're right, Rachel. I came in to see some old friends this weekend. I was supposed to go back today but some things got in the way and I decided to come and congratulate you. I'm proud your art is getting a lot of attention. I always knew you'd hit the big time someday." Jesse winked.

I'm glad he thinks so. I didn't hear that from Carter and it certainly is encouraging.

"Rachel, do you know anything about the work site? What is the big building in the center? Looks like JHR has big plans for that place." Jesse searched her face.

"Well, I was told that the big building in the center is a museum. In fact,

Return to Leiper's Fork

a gentleman approached me Saturday, during a lull and asked if I'd consider painting murals for it. I can see it now. There's a tree with an Indian peeking from behind it and Colonel Jesse Steed is riding his horse." Rachel's eyes danced with laughter.

Jesse pretended to be indignant. "Don't you dare make fun of my ancestors! If it weren't for them, I wouldn't be here. If I hear another word, I'll have to take those roses back to the florist." She heard his golden laugh. "What did you do with your painting, Rachel? I mean the one which hung over there?" He pointed to the empty space on the stone wall. Ignoring him, Rachel left the table to get dessert bowls. As she reached for them, Jesse was behind her. "Here, let me." As his arm brushed hers, Rachel stiffened but she could not deny how she felt when his large hand covered hers. She felt his warm breath on her neck. "Just let go and I'll hold them. I promise to not let them break. I always hold on tight when something is fragile and valuable." His hand tightened on hers.

I'm talking about you, Rachel. You're worth more than the world to me.

"Jesse, those bowls are so expensive, it would cost you two week's salary to replace them. Randall and I got them for a wedding gift but the China was too expensive for us to complete. Now, to answer your question. I sold the painting at the exhibit. You probably didn't notice it. I really didn't think it would happen but it did. It was very personal because I painted it months after Randall died. You see, I promised him I would do everything I could to keep Leiper's Fork from becoming commercially developed. I wanted it to stay the historic village it had always been. Rare, beautiful, quaint and different. It was hard when I saw the fields destroyed. I was so angry with you, because you sold us out. I didn't know what would happen to Leiper's Fork and our way of life. To many, we are hillbillies living in a one horse town. People think it's funny the way we sit on our porches in the evening drinking tea to soothe away the cares of the day but we're not taking drugs to sleep. Our country air puts babies to sleep and they don't need a pacifier. And those Christmas lights! People laugh when they see them strung up and down our two lane road but in Leiper's Fork, we celebrate Christmas all year long. It's not about gifts. It's about loving others and helping them. It's about community and being there for each other and our own families. It's preserving our way of life." She stopped to suck in her breath and glare at him. "There are some people who think they are so high and mighty, they would not only sell Leiper's Fork but their own soul if they thought they'd make a dollar profit."

Color tinged Jesse's cheeks. "I might have done that at one time, Rachel but not now. Money doesn't mean that much to me, anymore. I have more important business to attend to."

Such as pumping gas! Of course money doesn't mean much now. You're broke, Jesse.

As Jesse's eyes bored into hers, she turned away. When she looked up, she noticed his gray eyes blazing. His mouth formed a hard line. In almost a whisper, she continued, "I hated you Jesse, hated you for what you did. If you had not sold your land for God only knows what, those earthmoving vehicles wouldn't be scarring the country side. I don't know what else is going on down there. They keep the gates to the development locked. Everybody is guessing and no one is being told anything. I know one building will be a museum but what else I'm not sure about. Guess it's top secret, because Betsy told me they hired security twenty four hours a day. Imagine that! Anyway, my heart has softened just a bit since the reunion. I guess the old ticker is not as hard as it used to be." She touched his shoulder. "If it was, I wouldn't be serving you warm blackberry cobbler with ice cream. That is for sure." She laughed as she set the bowl in front of him but Jesse's appetite had waned. "You know Jesse, I couldn't save Leiper's Fork but I tried. I really tried. I even asked a judge in Nashville what I could do and he said, 'Protest and get arrested.' He said if you had zoning permits and you owned the land, I could do nothing about it. I had to give it to God but sometimes I'm not sure I'm over it."

Rachel. You don't know what you just said. You have so much power over me I turn to water every time I see you. If I was made of steel I would melt from your touch. What will happen when you find out what I have done behind your back? Will you destroy me again? What will I do when you marry Carter?

After dessert, they sat and talked a short time. Jesse didn't want to leave and Rachel dreaded the moment he would walk out the door. The hour was late and Jesse knew he would have to be at the airport for an early flight the next morning. "Rachel, I need to go. You look as tired as I feel. Thank you for supper. I know you thought I was crazy barging in here but I wanted to tell you how very proud I am of you. Finally, you got the recognition you deserved. This is just the beginning, you know. Great things are ahead. Good luck with your work at the museum."

Return to Leiper's Fork

"Now Jesse, I haven't been promised the job, yet. But thank you. What you said means a lot to me. If you ever need to borrow some m . . . money or anything, please call me. I'll always be there for you and that is a promise."

Jesse stepped closer. As Rachel reached up, he dropped a kiss on her forehead. "It's only a friend kiss, but I'd like to aim it farther south, honey. However, your engagement makes those lips off limits for now. However, I serve a God who said for me to call unto Him and He would show me great and marvelous things. So, I've been calling and waiting. I know He'll be faithful with his promises. How is that for a new Christian's faith? Keep your chin up, beautiful. I'll see you again, someday." He stepped on the porch with Rachel behind him.

"Jesse! When did you? I mean, how did it happen?" The shock on her face brought a smile to his.

"Rachel, let's just call it a miracle because that's what it was. I'm not who I used to be." She walked beside him, as a car careened around the curve and parked in front of the cabin. As they stood watching, Carter slammed his door and approached them.

"Rachel? Mr. Steed?" Carter stood with his hands on his hips in disbelief. "What is going on here? I come over here, to hopefully find my wallet and find instead, my fiancé with one of the college's trustees. Steed, I think if I were you, I'd leave immediately and Rachel, I believe you are going to do some answering. Meet me in the house fast!"

Rachel whispered, "Go, Jesse. I'll be okay. It will be alright."

"If you're afraid, leave with me now. I don't want you to stay. He's plenty angry." She saw the troubled look on Jesse's face.

From the porch, Carter yelled, "Rachel, you're taking your good time. Hurry up and get in here!" Jesse started striding toward the porch. His face was red and his eyes were angry. He couldn't dismiss the way Carter had spoken to Rachel.

"Go, Jesse! Please!" Rachel whispered hoarsely and hurried behind him.

Jesse hesitated. Should he leave or should he stay? Did he trust Carter to not hit her? Would he make things harder for Rachel if he confronted Carter? As they inched closer to the door, she whispered, "Don't Jesse! It will only make matters worse for me. Please go! Now!"

It was difficult to drive away and leave Rachel with a furious Carter but Jesse figured he might have made it more difficult if he had stayed. As he slowly drove past the cabin, he peered into the large bay window. Carter was standing over Rachel, as she held her head in her hands.

If Carter lays a hand on her, he'll pay forever. I'll tell Tony to see if she has any bruises when he meets with her tomorrow. If there is one mark on her body that will be the last woman Carter ever touches. My gut feeling about him is right and I know it. I just can't prove it.

With a tortured heart he drove on, That night his calls were answered.

Return to Leiper's Fork

Chapter 12: The Visitor

The next day, Rachel walked slowly up the stone steps to teach her class. Her shoulders hurt and she still had a headache but inside she was giddy. She had signed a contract with Tony Hunter. He'd been hired by the JHR Corporation to oversee the development of the Leiper's Fork site. The afternoon with Tony had been exciting as he talked with her about the museum. Rachel's mind raced with ideas. She had books about the history of Middle Tennessee and Leiper's Fork and after Tony left, she made quick sketches in a notebook.

Tony, a professional in his own right, said he had been given permission from corporate headquarters to interview her and offer a cash advance should she agree to quit her part time job and work each day and some evenings at the museum. An account would be opened in Nashville, in her name so she could purchase the supplies she would need. Although she regretted having to resign her job, Rachel wrote out her resignation, knowing Carter was going to be very unhappy with her. After last night, she didn't care. She didn't need Carter to save her home. Rachel smiled as she remembered the amount on the check. Thirty five thousand dollars was quite an advance and with her check from the exhibit on Saturday, she could pay off the loan on her cabin. She had already put in a call to the bank and now with the job at the museum, she could pay off her loan by Christmas. She wondered who had purchased, *The Promise*, and where it was hanging. Each time she thought of the painting she felt sorrowful.

I'll never see that painting again.

She hurried into the powder room to check her makeup. As she turned a corner, she overheard a conversation on the overhead balcony.

"Lil! For God's sake! Go back to Arkansas! What more do you want from me? I plan on marrying Rachel, soon." Rachel heard the desperation in Carter's voice but who was Lil?

"Carter, listen to me. How many times is history going to repeat itself? You move here, you move there. You fall in love with a woman half your age and I have to rescue you again and again. After Carol died, I got you into the hospital. I have loaned you money, which you never repay and another job and another city is not going to help you. You need medical help and this time, you're going to get it or you will never see another dime from me." The woman's voice sounded as if she meant business.

Rachel thought she heard a scuffle, then a slapping sound.

"Lil, if you grab me again, I'm going to backhand you and you know what I'm saying. I told you to not get me upset." The voice that had been threatening turned sorrowful. "I'm sorry, Lil. I shouldn't have hit you. I have a class waiting. I must go."

Rachel retreated back into the restroom and leaned her head against the cool tile wall. The pain in her upper arms and back was more than she could stand. She took out some aspirin and swallowed them.

I've had my doubts about Carter but now I know what I must do. Who is the woman with Carter and what was the conversation about changing jobs and being in the hospital? I know he hit her. Should I have intervened? Carter is a sick man. I must stay away from him.

As she peeped into the hall, she saw an elegantly dressed woman walk into Carter's office. Her hand was at the side of her face. Her blond hair was pulled back into a tight bun and a black suit covered her slender figure. Her only jewelry was a pair of pearl earrings and a matching necklace. Rachel thought she appeared to be in her late forties or mid-fifties. Could she be the person Carter was speaking with? Rachel decided to find out. She had a while before she needed the small auditorium Carter was using. Timidly, she approached the woman.

"Miss, I'm Rachel Benton, an instructor here. I think Carter, I mean, Dr. Viking, is teaching a class tonight. Is there some way I can help you?" As Rachel stepped into the office, the woman's pale violet eyes opened wide with surprise. Rachel watched as Lil slowly removed her thick tortoise shell glasses and studied her from head to foot. Rachel noticed a bright red spot forming on the woman's cheek. As Rachel looked around, she thought Carter's office was as impeccable as he was. In fact, she thought it was

Return to Leiper's Fork

picture perfect _ not like the office of any professor she had ever known. She noticed a large signed painting on the wall and walked toward it. Lil joined her. She knew Carter had a fiancé but never dreamed she'd meet her.

"Quite magnificent isn't it?" The woman met Rachel's gaze boldly, while touching the gold ornate frame. "One of Carter's best, I think. More than likely . . . his last." As Rachel got closer, she thought the painting was gaudy. The swirling greens and blues screamed at her and as she peered at the signature, alarms went off inside her.

Reminds me of Van Gogh's, Starry Night and it gave me a headache.

Rachel responded slowly. "This is the first time I've seen this painting. I have never been in Carter's office." She nervously twisted her hands behind her back. For some reason, she felt like a storm was beginning to brew. She knew she had better guard every word she said.

The woman wearing heavy makeup turned toward her. "I'm Lil Young, Dean of Fine Arts, University of Arkansas. So, you are the woman, engaged to Carter." As she slowly opened her brightly colored lips, it appeared to Rachel she was forcing herself to smile. The scene reminded Rachel of a python before it began squeezing its prey. Even the temperature in the room felt cooler. Rachel shivered as Miss Young reached out a thin arm to draw her closer. Her long manicured nails reminded Rachel of a vulture's long grasping talons slowly closing around a helpless prey.
Rachel wanted to run but felt frozen to the floor.

"Please don't be anxious my dear. I am glad we have time to chat. I don't know how serious you are about Carter but truly, darling, I hope you've not purchased your wedding dress. If you have, I hope you kept your receipt." She offered a shallow laugh. "You see, Carter has a habit of falling in and out of love with almost every young thing he meets. Sometimes, he even asks them to marry him." Lil lifted her head and laughed cruelly before turning back to a stunned Rachel. "Carter is a very intelligent and handsome man but he has one fault. He is totally irresponsible when it comes to taking care of someone and after a while he walks away and runs back to me, especially when the money dries up. I believe an intelligent woman such as you would not want that to happen. I'm here to save him before his next fall. He's had several women friends since his wife died and I know that for sure. You see, Carter and I go a long way back. I was the first Mrs. Viking. It didn't last long, especially after I stuck my neck out to get him a job. I've always been there to help him when he couldn't help himself and I'm not sure why I do it. I guess deep down, I not only love him in some sick way but I know I am the only one left to help him." Rachel was not sure if to feel more sorry for Lil or for Carter but she knew both needed professional help.

As she groped for the nearest chair, Lil laughed shrilly. She looked down at Rachel and pointed her finger. "I can see surprise written all over your pretty little face but let's cut to the chase. He presented you with a large pear shaped diamond and told you, he sold his house in Little Rock, didn't he?" Rachel thought Lil's laugh was more a ghostly shriek, than a human sound. Lil slowly examined her nails before continuing. "That house he told you about belongs to me and when life gets stressful, that's where he comes to stay, until he gets better and resorts to roaming again. Miss Benton, am I correct when I say he wanted to marry you right away?"

Rachel nodded, numbly. "Yes, Miss Young. You are correct."

"Listen, I've known Carter for years. Honey, he is a chameleon. He changes colors when he needs to. Carter is not for you, child. He is arrogant, proud, demanding, jealous, angry and lousy with money. He uses women to build his aging ego. When he tires of them, he tosses them aside, like a rag doll. He was married two years ago for a while. It seems his wife had a bad accident. It was ruled suicidal but the police had questions. Carter is good at what he does but he is a very sick man. I have got him out of situation after situation and if you have a brain in that pretty little head of yours, you'll break that engagement as fast as you can. You see, that ring you have on your finger belonged to his wife." Rachel gasped as the diamond winked at her. Lil continued, as Rachel held the sparkling gem mounted in platinum, in her hand. "Carter kept it in a deposit box, in Little Rock until he needed it."

As Rachel stood dumbfounded, footsteps sounded from down the hall and halted at the office door. A shocked Carter stepped inside his office.
"Lil! What are you doing here? I mean, I thought you left. Rachel!" His eyes went from one to the other. His words echoed in the silence. "I hoped you two would never meet."

Carter licked his lips, as disbelief showed in his eyes. Rachel looked first at the man who was somewhere between shock and anger and then at Lil Young. "Here, Carter. You might need this for your next conquest." She placed the engagement ring in his shaking hand then turned to the woman near her. "Miss Young, I owe you a great debt and for some strange reason, I believe you. Good bye, Carter."

Anguish filled Carter's eyes. "Wait, Rachel! I can explain everything. Don't leave me, honey. I need you. I must have you." Carter reached out to her.

With a courage and confidence, she did not know she possessed, Rachel faced him. Her voice was calm but her eyes blazed. "You don't need me, Carter. You need Miss Young. She's more willing to nurse you than I am. By the way, do not call and do not visit or I'll have you arrested by Sheriff Adams. Am I making myself clear?"

A stricken Carter nodded his head, as Rachel retrieved an envelope from her purse. "Good! I hope I never see you again. This is the letter of resignation I was going to give you, tonight. You understand now, why I cannot work with you again. Goodbye."

Lil cradled Carter's head in her hands. "Lil! What is going to happen to me? Things were going so well and I do love Rachel." Soft whimpering sounds filled the room as Rachel backed out the door.

Lil slowly lifted Carter's head and searched his sad eyes. "There, there dear. I've always taken care of you. I'll get you back to Arkansas as soon as possible. We'll have to obtain a medical leave but I can pull those strings. I'll take care of all of that in the morning. First I need to get you to your apartment." Lil's voice was soft and soothing. "Nothing is too hard for us, darling. I only want to take care of you."

Rachel grabbed a marker and raced to the auditorium before fleeing the building. Later, the students found a note on the auditorium door.

CLASS CANCELLED UNTIL FURTHER NOTICE.

Chapter 13: Yard Sales

Rachel was proud that the murals were finally coming together. She had sketched Indians and portrayed their daily life in the Middle Tennessee region. Tomorrow, she would begin painting the settlers who came to the Leiper's Fork area. Tony Hunter was as proud as a new father, as he looked at Rachel's progress. He thought about asking her to dinner, as she headed toward the door but he knew better. Rachel Benton was off limits for more than one reason. He watched her drive out of the parking lot. As she approached the highway, she noticed a truck towing away a car from the Steed property.

Evidently, Jesse has more financial woes than I ever dreamed. I guess he's barely making a living pumping gas. In fact, he must really be suffering financially, to sell his antique car.

She ached remembering that she was to ride in that car with Jesse to the senior prom. She had ended up going with Randall and Jesse has asked Susanna. Their lives changed drastically after that.

Rachel drove home troubled. How could she help Jesse without making him feel worse? She knew he would never borrow money from her. She guessed he was financing his plane tickets by selling his father's car.

As she painted that week, footsteps sounded behind her. After waiting a few seconds she turned around to see someone gazing up at her. "Jesse! What are you doing here?"

"Right now, I'm admiring a work of art which has nothing to do with the paint on the wall." He smiled and lifted his arms. "If Rapunzel would let me have her paintbrush, I'd help her climb down the ladder. In fact, I'd take her to lunch. Mighty fine eating at Puckett's today. In fact, burgers are calling our names." He checked his watch and looked at her tenderly. "If you could spare an hour, I'd buy lunch. I get tired of eating junk food from the station." He chuckled, as Rachel feigned a look of pity. "Just think, Miss Benton. Those fat fries are calling our names." For some reason having him there made Rachel the happiest she had been in a while.

Return to Leiper's Fork

"Jesse, I don't look very presentable right now. You know with all this paint here and there." Rachel inspected her clothing, noting smears of paint on her jeans. "Besides . . ."

"Besides, nothing! I know you're engaged but that should not keep you from eating. I'm sure Carter doesn't want to see a stick bride coming down the aisle. At least, I wouldn't." He sighed and stood back exasperated.

"Well, how about letting me pay you back for the supper I had, the last time I was in town? That was a great meal and I can't forget the blackberry cobbler. By the way, how's that finger doing?"

Rachel examined her finger. "I can't tell it was ever burned."

"Let the Boy Scout see for himself. Come down a few more steps and I'll help you." As he placed his hands at her waist and swung her to the floor, Jesse knew she felt lighter than she'd felt before. He breathed in the sweet scent of her hair that reminded him of sweet lavender and held her tighter than he should have. been called back to Tennessee but it didn't have anything to do with French fries or Puckett's fried chicken.

After standing her securely on the floor, he examined her finger. "Come to think of it, I believe my Boy Scout first aide training finally came in handy. You look fine to me, princess. So let's go get those burgers and fries. I might throw in a milkshake, if you'd bat those beautiful black lashes at me. I'd feel like a million dollars."

Rachel looked him in the eyes. "Jesse, I will go with you on one condition. I buy lunch."

It probably took every penny he made to get to Leiper's Fork.

"No way, Rachel. My dad taught me a gentleman always pays for a lady's lunch. If I didn't have the money, I wouldn't be inviting you."

"Shouldn't you be working?"

"We had to quit pumping gas. Seems we have a problem at the location and I was given the week off. It's about regulations. You know the usual stuff. Rachel looked at him strangely. What would be so difficult about pumping gas? "They gave me a week's vacation with pay and my friend brought me in his plane. Never cost me a dime." He turned away and changed the subject.

"I'm borrowing Bud's truck, so let's get on down the highway. I'm so hungry I could eat trees."

As they munched burgers, Jesse noticed Rachel's hand. "What's your fiancé going to say about that bare finger? The jeweler didn't come get his ring, did he?" Jesse chuckled to himself, as he dipped a fry in catsup. "I wouldn't keep that diamond off too long if you know what I mean. I think you know Carter is the jealous type." He munched the fry, and casually sipped his soda, all the while knowing the look she was giving him would freeze hot grease on Ron's grill.

Rachel's smoky, dark eyes spoke volumes. "That is a very sore subject, Jesse. I'm not sure how to answer that question. Let's just say I changed my mind and I thank God it's over.

Hallelujah! You bet your paint palette and brushes it's over. I hadn't heard the news about the broken engagement but I heard he left the college with the dean in tow.

"Jesse, I guess you are still a trustee at the college, so I might as well tell you, I gave Carter back his ring. The last I heard, he had resigned his position. I also, resigned mine. I guess the Fine Arts Department is sort of in limbo now but thank goodness for others who stepped in. I knew when I broke the engagement, Carter would have me fired. That's why I wrote out my resignation. I also needed more time to paint the murals. Thank God, it all worked out. Mrs. Claremont told me, Carter went back to Arkansas. Thank you for helping me. I realize you could not tell me everything but you did open my eyes. In some sad way, I am glad I met Lil Young even though I feel sorry for her." She searched Jesse's gray eyes. Did he understand how much she owed him? She shuddered to think she could have married Carter, if Jesse had not intervened. "Jesse, I need to thank Tony Hunter for hiring me. If he had not showed up the day of the exhibit, I don't know what I would have done financially. He is a dear, dear man but oh so shy. He won't even eat lunch with me."

No darling. Tony Hunter had nothing to do with hiring you and he knows better than eat lunch with the woman I love.

"Rachel, I had questions about Carter. After we did a background check, there were some things I could not get out of my mind. There were too many questions about him and my gut feeling was that something was not right. You didn't know anything about it and I couldn't tell. His wife had a few bruises on her that didn't make sense and her head trauma was attributed to falling down the steps. The coroner labeled it an accident but it couldn't be proven. She died and also lost her unborn baby. Personally, I think he has an anger problem and he caused the accident. Carter was a very prominent educator, and Miss Young had plenty of money to battle for him in court. He's a very sick man and if I have anything to do with it, he'll never work in a college again."

"Jesse! If I had only known! Carter scared me. When you left me that night, I wanted to go with you but I was afraid he'd come after you later. He was so relieved to get his wallet back that he left right after . . . right after . . ." Rachel looked away. "I'm just glad he's gone. So glad! Now, I can sleep nights." She rubbed the aching muscles in her shoulders as Jesse looked at her strangely.

He touched her hand. "Do you like your new job, Rachel?" Today, she was more beautiful than the night at the exhibit. Her faded jeans and red plaid blouse made her appear eighteen rather than a woman in her late twenties. She was the picture of innocence and country beauty combined and Jesse was bothered. This was a woman he would never forget, regardless of what happened in their lives. At the same time, his life was changing and one day he would have to say goodbye to Leiper's Fork.

Make the most of your good times with her, Jesse. They're almost over.

Rachel put her hand on his. "Jesse, you're looking mighty serious. What are you thinking? Have I kept you here too long?" She grabbed her purse and pushed back her chair.

"Oh no, Rachel! I couldn't be happier. Being at home and having lunch with you, means a lot to me. Maybe more than you know."

Driving back to the work site, Jesse asked if she would go with him on the eighty-four mile yard sale the next morning. "You know, it's time you had a rest and Bud said if we went, we could use his truck. You never know what we might find from here to Kentucky. Wonder who ever thought of a yard sale eighty-four miles long. I've got the day and we can start at eight o'clock in the morning. It ends at dusk. If we get tired we can turn around and come back home. What do you say, Pork Princess?" He dared to hope she would go with him.

"All I've got to say, Mr. Steed is, Oink, oink!' Rachel could not quit laughing, so Jesse poked her lightly in the ribs.

"Is that all you've got to say, Pork Princess, because if you continue teasing me, I might have to turn you into chops, or little sausages. Seriously, I think you've been working too hard. Looks like you might have lost a little weight, so you need to be treated royally."

Rachel ignored his comment about losing weight. Carter had kept reminding her that she needed to be thinner before the wedding. "Turn me into chops or sausage. Hmmm! Is that a threat, Mr. Steed?" Rachel pretended offense.

He looked at her and shook his head slightly. "It will be, if you don't spend the day with me. That's all I'm asking, Rachel. Take pity on a poor man who leads a dull life and needs a little fun. You just broke your engagement, so I'm not asking you to marry me. It's too soon to be serious, so don't think for a minute this is a pre-nup dinner. I'm way too busy to be tied down, so don't consider me fresh bacon." Rachel could not hold back her laugh. What fun she had with Jesse. Compared to Carter, he was relief spelled with a capital R. Rachel watched as a smile played on Jesse's face then felt him touch her hand. "Don't take anything I said, seriously. You know me better than that."

Rachel, if you were ready, I'd be the happiest man in Williamson County. I only wish we were headed to Charleston for a honey moon instead of going on a yard sale for the next eighty four miles.

"Jesse, when I started seeing behaviors I didn't appreciate, I knew I had to cut my ties with Carter. He was a very impatient man. There were times, I was afraid to be with him but I couldn't ask you to intervene and I didn't know how to break it off because I needed the job."

"Honey, I would have gladly intervened in your behalf and I'm glad you didn't marry him. You don't know what a relief it was to hear you'd broken your engagement."

Return to Leiper's Fork

Early the next morning, two happy people set out to spend a day on the eighty-four mile yard sale. After hours of looking and Rachel refusing to let Jesse pay for her purchases, they decided to find a quiet place and eat the picnic lunch Rachel had prepared.

"Fried chicken like this is hard to find, Miss Benton." Jesse bit into a drumstick and smacked his lips, as Rachel reached over to wipe them. She hesitated, as he looked into her eyes. Both were aware of their closeness. Moments went by and Rachel finally looked away. Jesse pretended nothing had happened. "Thanks, gorgeous. In my haste I didn't know that dribbles were on my chin. I'm probably making a pig of myself but I didn't know how hungry I was. That potato salad isn't bad either, not to mention what I'm going to do when you hand me that piece of carrot cake. Although I do try to eat healthy, I never turn down black berry cobbler or a nice piece of cake." He flexed his muscles. "Got to stay fit you know, in case a bear comes around. In seconds, bears can sniff out beautiful women but don't you worry, I've got on my Spider Man suit under these duds." Jesse pointed to his shirt and reached for a slice of cake covered with pecans.

Rachel was silent, as she looked around. "Jesse, are you kidding? Do you really think a bear might be around here? If you do, I'm running to the car. It can have all this food." Panic filled Rachel's eyes. She had heard of bears in the wilds of Tennessee and how they attacked from nowhere. Once she had seen tourists taking pictures of a bear, when it was only feet away.

"Well, it could happen but not likely on a weekend like this. The poor bears are afraid to come out of hiding. Some women might try to buy their fur coats." He laughed and flexed his muscles again. "Imagine that! A bear being cheated out of his fur! But honey, never fear. Steed is here!" He chuckled as Rachel slapped his arm.

"Jesse! I've never been afraid when you were around."

His cell rang and Rachel watched as disappointment swept across his face. After the call, he slowly placed the cell in his pocket and heaved a long sigh. Rachel swatted flies which were stealing cake crumbs from the blanket.

"Mr. Hero, you might finish your lunch. Everybody else is getting those bargains except us." Rachel jumped up but Jesse grabbed her hand.

"Just a minute, Rachel. One day I hope to tell you how much you mean to me but this is not the time. I came to Nashville with one of my best friends, who is a pilot. His daughter is expecting her baby any minute. Seems his wife has already taken her to the hospital and his son-in-law is on his way, to be by her side. First time parents, you know. My friend has to leave by four o'clock. I'm sorry to cut our time short but we've got to start back. Don't worry about anything, Bud or one of the men can take me to the airport."

Jesse pulled her to her feet after seeing her disappointment. "Sorry to ruin your day, beautiful, after all you've done." He pointed to the remains of their lunch." I'll make it up to you as soon as I can but I don't know when that will be. Would Thanksgiving be okay?"

"Jesse! That is six weeks away! I guess I can get those turkey and Indian murals painted during that time. Mom and Dad are having friends over and she's asked me to help her. If you don't have any place special to go, come to Mom's. I think dinner will be at two o'clock and we'll set an extra plate for you. She wouldn't hear of having dinner at the cabin. Said she wanted to have it in her house, as long as she possibly could. "

"Rachel, if all I had was a fried bologna sandwich, it would be a feast if I could be with you. But don't worry. I'll make it home before you can stuff that turkey." Jesse gave her a kiss and embraced her tightly before getting in the truck and turning toward Leiper's Fork.

That evening, Rachel enjoyed looking over the treasures she had collected at the yard sales. She had laughed when Jesse complained about carrying her bundles. "Jesse Steed, why do you think God gave men broad shoulders?" Without waiting for a response, she continued. "To carry a woman's purchases, that's why!" Her laughter reminded him of tiny bells tinkling in a soft breeze.

Jesse had responded in the same manner. "Rachel, there's only one problem. That responsibility comes only with a marriage certificate. That could be settled anytime you get ready. Honey, I'd be delighted to carry your purchases for the rest of your life." He chuckled while watching her face turn pink. "Just tell me when you get ready and I'll be glad to purchase

Return to Leiper's Fork

the license.

"Jesse, I'm not buying much." Rachel looked at him nervously.

She slowly examined the worn, monogrammed linens. They'd be fine after they were washed. She'd use them someday for a luncheon. Her main treasure was a small walnut cabinet with two carved side shelves and a pull out drawer. It was a man's shaving cabinet with a mirror and a drawer for a comb and razor. She would hang it in the guest bathroom. The lady from whom she'd purchased it, said it had belonged to her father and he had made it when she was five years old. Rachel knew it was old because the woman said she was over ninety years now. Jesse grunted when he lifted it to his shoulder. Walnut was heavy. "Woman, I'm just lucky you didn't buy an oak pie safe." He gave her a swat and playfully grunted his way to the car.

"Now, Mr. Steed, you are finally sounding like a Pork Princess's date."

Chapter 14: The Conversation

Rachel continued painting day after day and soon the murals were finished. In the course of a conversation, Tony told her he was from Seattle and had known Jesse for many months. It was through their friendship and love of art that Jesse hired Tony as his curator. Rachel invited him to dinner one night but at the last minute he said he had to go to Nashville for a meeting. Handsome Tony Hunter would be quite a catch but he didn't seem to care about being caught. .

The amphitheater was nearly complete and the landscapers were finishing their work. Come spring, everything would be in full bloom. The theater in the museum was close to completion and the large red barn was ready with the finest sound system money could buy. A log cabin had been built and wax figures were waiting to be placed at the last minute. The wax family in one wagon could have been mistaken for real people and so could the Indians in full dress holding fish they had caught in the creek near the cabin that boasted a fireplace.

The Chamber of Commerce was anxious for a ribbon cutting and Tony made sure everything would be ready for the big day. It was rumored the JHR corporate heads would descend on Leiper's Fork for the dedication and Tony and his workmen were making sure the most minute details were complete. As Rachel looked around her, she knew JHR Corporation had poured millions into this project. She shook her head in amazement, as she thought how much it would cost for families to visit the grounds. Even the gift shop was loaded with numerous items to purchase and boxes were arriving each day. "This corporation will try to squeeze every dollar they can from us. Then they'll fly around the world to their vacation homes and laugh at the little man who filled their pockets with his hard earned money. But I need to be more grateful. They gave me a job when I needed one."

Days raced by and fall nipped the heels of summer. Days became shorter and red and gold leaves of the maple trees rustled in the breeze and twirled and whirled to the hills and vales below. Leiper's Fork was settling in for winter and Thanksgiving Day would soon be upon them. Orange Corn flowers faded and Black Eyed Susans nodded their heads. Gray

Return to Leiper's Fork

squirrels were busy gathering nuts and securing their leafy winter homes in the tall, oak trees. Sourwoods shed their lacy skirts of white and wrapped themselves in deep dark shawls. Rachel watched as her hydrangea lost its blush and bent its head, knowing winter would soon blow away blossoms that had long dried on branches. Rachel also dressed for fall knowing her colorful warm sweaters and scarves would feel good against the evening's cold.

She wondered what Jesse was doing and where he was. She had not heard from him in three weeks. One day she visited her parents for supper and took a walk in the woods. She wanted to see the tree trunk where she and Jesse had carved their initials ten years before. She noticed several trees had fallen but continued searching for the one tree that bore their initials. After her father returned, she questioned him about its disappearance.

"Daughter, I've cut a lot of them trees down. Getting ready for winter, you know. I'm sorry but I never really gave a thought about it. I have to split logs for winter fuel. Now, you'll get over it. That's stuff young'uns do, then grow up and forget. Your warm stove will feel real good when the snow flies. By the way, I'll bring you over a cord of wood for your fireplace. You'll enjoy drinking a cup of hot coffee in front of the fire, when everybody is trying to get up and down Hillsboro Road in the snow." Bill Locke reached out to embrace his only child. "Buck up, honey. I know it's lonely around here with Jesse gone but he'll be back one day. He told me so."

Time passed slowly and one day, as Rachel was taking a break, she overheard two workmen talking. Evidently, they had stopped for a coffee break. She was so near, she could hear them opening their thermoses. As they sipped their coffee and fell into conversation, she couldn't help but hear Jesse's name. That's when her ears perked up.

"Jesse Steed own this place?

"Well, don't rightly know. What makes you think that?" The workman took a bite of his snack cake and a long drink of his coffee.

"Heard Bud telling some guy in a suit the other day that Jesse had the final say so in everything that went on here. From what I know, he's the money behind all of this, too. Besides, I saw the UPS man come in here and leave some yellow envelopes from Canada, for Jesse, the same day he left with that woman, who's doing those murals. Later, Jesse rushed in here like a wild fire and him and Bud took out and went to the airport. Ain't seen Jesse, since." Rachel could hardly believe her ears.

"Thought he lost everything he owned, back in the summer."

"Bud Lee reports to him or so it seems. One day I saw a paper on the counter and it had Jesse Steed's address in Seattle. He had signed off on the cost of moving the old school house, not to mention the cost of the landscaping and concrete work. If he was so broke, how come he's got anything and everything to do with this place? A whole lot of money is going to be spent here before it's over. Did you see that rose garden out there with that huge sundial in it? Them iron benches around it ain't cheap. They are made down there in Marietta, Georgia and how about that theater? The lighting and sound equipment would break King Solomon. I'll tell you something, by gum. This place is a state of the art museum, if I say so."

The worker in the blue ball cap took a sip of his coffee, wiped his mouth on his sleeve and continued. "Well, what you're saying makes sense. The fountain isn't finished yet and that's going to be something else, not to mention that huge barn over in the field where the bands will perform. Leiper's Fork is going to be on the map for sure when everybody sees what Jesse has done here. Why, we'll run Nashville right off the map." The men let out a roar of laughter that would have scared a mountain lion. "Man, the next thing you know, there's going to be hotels and gas stations springing up all over this town. Jesse will probably rake in the big money then. You know it takes money to make money and I wish I had just a little bit more to spend myself. You know this economy has about done us all in."

Rachel's heart skipped a beat, as her blood pressure rose. Jesse had betrayed her with lies and his secret ambition to make millions off of Leiper's Fork. He'd not lost the Steed fortune after all. He was a business man who preyed on others _ a vulture more than likely. Blindly, she escaped down the hall and sat outdoors underneath the overcast sky. The day had been dismal enough without overhearing the men's conversations. She pulled her sweater around her and looked up at the same dreariness she'd witnessed the day of Randall's burial. The Canadian Geese high overhead flew in formation and honked their sympathies to the woman

Return to Leiper's Fork

hunched on the stone bench.

Gray day! Gray sky! Gray geese! Gray clouds! This day can't get much more depressing. Jesse, you've got a lot of explaining to do if those men have their stories correct.

After buttoning her sweater, Rachel felt the wind catch up her golden, brown hair and lash it against her face. "That's the punishment I deserve for trusting Jesse." For several minutes she lifted her face and searched the heavens for answers, while the cold winter wind, dried her face.

"So, Jesse Steed is behind all of this. I should have known better. How he must have laughed when I left a twenty dollar bill in Bud's car, to pay for the gas the day we went to the yard sales. I don't know if I am angry or appointed but I'd like to slap his handsome face. He has certainly made me look like a fool but I allowed myself to be caught up in his schemes. I set out to protect Leiper's Fork and got snared in the process by Jesse and his big money. He's a lot smarter than I am."

Wiping her face quickly, Rachel went to finish her work. She wanted to get away but she had a lot to accomplish before December. One more week until Thanksgiving and she would have to face Jesse. Would he return to Leiper's Fork for the holidays? She hoped with all of her heart he would get lost in an airport and never find his way to Leiper's Fork.

There is no fury like a woman's fury. Jesse Steed will finally meet his match when he returns and he'll wish he had never come home for Thanksgiving dinner when he sees what I am going to serve him.

Feverishly, she painted the mural of Puckett's Store, The Old Country Restaurant, Leiper's Fork Gallery and numerous other businesses, including, The Barn, a gallery where the owner claimed horses could stick their heads inside his windows. Barney Fife's police car took center stage and Rachel laughed as she painted Christmas lights along Old Hillsboro Road. When the last drop of paint was dry, she stood back to view her work. How she loved her tiny village! As she stood below the murals, the story of Leiper's Fork came to life in the drawing. She had painted the faces of tired settlers arriving in wagons from Virginia and North Carolina and Indians from the region watching them. She painted the felled trees from which cabins rose and the animals they would kill for food. The Middle Tennessee Railroad came to life and as it rounded the bend of Leiper's

Fork, Rachel caught her breath. It was on those tracks that Jesse declared his love and kissed her. Later, they carved their initials in the tree and swore their love to each other forever.

"If you will marry me, I will give you Leiper's Fork."

"Jesse, you can't give me this town. It belongs to the people."

"Wait and see, Rachel. Wait and see. I believe marriage is forever and you were made for me. I have a dream and one day I will see it fulfilled. It will be a gift to our town and to you. One day I want my children to grow up here. This is our home, our way of life. We have to go to college but one day we'll return and sit on our porch and locate the constellations, while the kids catch fireflies. On weekends we'll dance at The Fork, and on Sundays we'll go to church and come home to fried chicken and all the fixings." He sighed and took her hand in his. "One day it will happen. I promise you that."

"Jesse, I won't forget what you said and I will give you my answer by graduation. I can't imagine life without you. I don't take marriage lightly because it is a commitment to God and a commitment to each other forever."

Return to Leiper's Fork

Chapter 15: Thanksgiving

Thanksgiving Day finally arrived. Rachel and her mother baked pies, prepared salads and kept the turkey under foil until half past two. Talk about the weather and the economy finally grew into silence. Rachel paced the floor and looked out the front door but there was no sign of Jesse.

"He's coming honey. I know he is. Probably ran into something he couldn't do anything about. You know how those long lines are at the airports." Her mother patted her on the back and told her to repair her makeup. "When that boy comes through the door, I want him to see what a beauty you are. No wonder he can't get over you. You're simply glowing today."

"Mom, I haven't told you everything that has been on my mind. When Jesse comes, it won't be, 'Jesse how about a piece of Mom's blueberry pie? Would you like another hot roll?' What I have to say will not make for a happy Thanksgiving." Mrs. Locke looked at her daughter sharply, wondering if it had been a good idea to invite Jesse to dinner. She wondered what had happened between the two, since Jesse left.

At three, the family gave up waiting and decided to enjoy the platters and bowls of food which covered the table. As Mr. Locke lifted up the prayer, Rachel's mind was on Jesse. Did he forget her invitation? Was he somewhere more exciting than Leiper's Fork? Had he lied when he accepted the invitation? Did he even care about her anymore? After dinner, Rachel pleaded a headache and left for home. Each time her phone rang, she was sure it was Jesse but after a few hours, gave up hope.

Rachel dozed on the sofa in the evening and watched as dark shadows filled the cabin. How she had looked forward to Jesse coming home for Thanksgiving dinner. She had planned a cozy evening at the cabin and even iced a dozen cupcakes. All at once, light flashed across her walls and a car quickly turned into her driveway. She heard footsteps on her porch and counted the seconds until she heard a rapping on the door, all the while holding her breath. At first, she thought it was her parents coming to see if she was okay but she remembered hearing only one person on the porch. Bill Locke walked slowly so it couldn't be him. Could Jesse have come after all? She wasn't sure of her feelings.

As she opened the door, Jesse stood with blood shot eyes and lines of fatigue written on his face. After seeing her disappointment, he spoke slowly. "I'm sorry, Rachel. Truly sorry. This has been the worse Thanksgiving, I have ever experienced, but I tried." Placing his hands along her face, he whispered hoarsely, "I've missed you, honey." He searched her lips with his, but she jerked away.

"Jesse! We waited for you. Waited until three o'clock! What happened?" As he drew her into the shelter of his arms, her anger and loneliness began to melt. He murmured her name over and over and pressed his face in the hollow of her neck. He had truly missed her. Rachel prayed for help.

"My precious, precious sweetheart. I didn't make it for dinner but I did make it to see you." He breathed heavily against her and held her tighter. It felt so right. "All of the craziness of the day was worth it, just to be with you but I'll tell you about it later. Right now, I am starving. Wouldn't have brought some of your mom's good cooking home, would you? I sure hope so. I've been thinking about, Cherry Berries on a Cloud, all day. I can taste it now." The hungry man smacked his lips and headed for the kitchen.

After she filled a plate with mashed potatoes, turkey, dressing and cold salad, Rachel sat down at the table. She watched him for a few moments knowing it felt so right to see him in her home. "Mr. Steed, you definitely are one hungry man. How about a hot cup of coffee and some of that dessert you talked about? I also baked chocolate cupcakes for you. Afternoons can be lonely when you're waiting for someone to arrive."

Jesse licked his lips. A warm fire, a beautiful woman and lots of delicious food. What more could a man want? He had an innocent look on his face, as he stuck his finger in the cherry topping and placed a cherry on Rachel's nose.

"Jesse! Stop that right now!" Rachel feigned anger but knew Jesse was having fun.

"Jesse Steed. You crazy man!" They both laughed. He licked off the cherry and took a chance by moving his lips one inch south.

My heart loves this man but how can he act so innocent and loving when he has betrayed me all these months? Jesse has been shrewd, deceptive and greedy. How will this night end?

After the late meal, they relaxed on the sofa in front of the fireplace.
"Honey, this is what a man needs. A hot meal in a beautiful home with a warm fire and a loving woman. I am tired of spending holidays alone. It's the loneliest feeling in the world, when families are together laughing and eating and I don't have anyone. Rachel, do you understand what I'm saying? More than that, can you tell me what I've been waiting ten years to hear? Do you love me as much as I love you? I tried to forget you but I couldn't. I love you more than life itself." As he searched her face for the answer he wanted and needed to hear, her eyes mocked his.

"Jesse, before I can tell you, I love you, I need some answers. Will you tell me the truth?"

Jesse blanched. "The truth? Rachel, I apologized for being late. I had no control over the airports and their flight schedules."

"No, Jesse. I'm not talking about you being late and flight schedules. I can understand that. However you could have called. That would have been the decent thing to do."

Jesse placed his fingers to her lips. "First things first, Rachel. Let me talk and you listen. The plane was late leaving SeaTac because of a snow storm. We had seven inches and the runway had to be cleaned. Planes were coming in and circling for hours because they had no place to land. The planes on the ground could not lift off. Babies were crying and some woman went crazy because she was missing Thanksgiving with her family. Soldiers were standing around and they'd just arrived from Afghanistan and couldn't get out of Seattle. I tried to call you but my battery must have died. I couldn't get your number because it was in my phone. Nowhere could I get it fixed and I was more agitated than you could imagine. When we got to Phoenix, there was a layover for three hours and after a while, I gave up hoping I'd get here for dinner. I will apologize to your mother tomorrow but I absolutely could not help being late. Besides, I didn't have your mother's number if I could have got to a phone booth. I tried to call Bud but had to leave him a message. After we landed in Nashville, I rented a car and broke the speed limit but I made it, as you can see. Your parents had already gone to bed so I drove on over here. If I told you I am sorry a thousand times, would it do any good?" A sadness engulfed him and it was apparent on his face as Rachel searched his eyes.

"Jesse. I'm so sorry you had to go through all that and miss dinner. I never dreamed you were having such a horrible time. I forgive you for that. You couldn't help it. But that's not what's bothering me. I have questions that have nothing to do with your trip and I hope you will be honest with me. I really need to talk with you about that in order for us to go on." Rachel exhaled and hugged her arms to her. This conversation was going to be difficult.

Jesse whispered, "So you have a few questions you need to ask, honey?"

Rachel looked at him then folded her hands in her lap. "Love is built on trust and respect. If that foundation isn't there, there is no chance for a marriage and especially a lasting one."

Jesse nodded in agreement. "I'm with you on that." He waited quietly for Rachel to continue but she hesitated for a few moments. "Well Rachel, I'm ready anytime you are. I don't know what this is all about but I'm willing to listen." Jesse exhaled and stretched his arms over his head. "Just spill your guts Rachel. I'll take whatever you dish out. I guess I can handle another problem after all of the ones I've had today. I can see your frustration." Finally, he stood to his feet, rubbing his eyes.

"Jesse, you've deceived me. You told me you pumped gas for a living and I believed you. We thought you lost everything when the economy went south. You even had to sell your father's car. I know! I saw it being towed from your driveway." At his piercing glance, she stopped and caught her breath and pushed back a wayward curl. "When I overheard a conversation that you owned the development site and were the money behind the construction, I knew you'd lied to me. You had Tony hire me but I didn't need your pity, Jesse. Was I really good enough for the job or did it matter? You knew if I left the college, I wouldn't have a job. I'm sure you were the one who decided on the amount of the advance, weren't you? You knew I'd lose the house and you felt sorry for me. That's hard, Jesse. All that time, I thought it was my ability that got me the job. It was you and

Return to Leiper's Fork

to find that out crushes me." Rachel covered her face. Her trembling shoulders broke Jesse's heart. Haltingly she spoke. "Did you arrange f . . .for my paintings to be a part of the exhibit, Jesse?"

Never had a man suffered so much, who'd tried to do so much good. At that time, Jesse thought a bullet through his chest would have been more merciful. As he reached out to her, Rachel cried out, "It was all too good to be true wasn't it? You lied to me and you kept everything secret, so you could make a lot of money. You're all about money aren't you? That's the bottom line but it has nothing to do with happiness. You tried to buy me didn't you? If you could get me away from Carter, you could have me all to yourself, then I would be eternally grateful for you saving me. If it had not been for Miss Young, I would have doubted everything you ever told me about Carter Viking. That's how much I trust you, Jesse." Rachel laid her head in her hands, as tears fell into her lap. "I didn't care that you lost everything. I would have married you because I loved you. I would have lived in a shack in the backwoods with you, but not now! I've seen the real Jesse Steed and he makes me sick! Greed is going to destroy you, Jesse, but it will never destroy me because I don't worship the almighty dollar. I want you to leave now. Get out of my house!"

Jesse's face was ashen, as he challenged her eyes and moved toward the door. "You had your say and I'm going to have mine. Little Lady, I may have kept a few secrets but maybe I had a very good reason. I don't think I owe you or anyone else an explanation as to why I've done what I've done. Business men don't have to tell everything they're doing if their heart is in the right place and you'd better believe Miss Benton, my heart is in the right place. If it wasn't, do you think God would hear my prayers every day? Do you think I could hold up my head if I was beating everyone out of their last dollar? That's greed with a capital G." He sighed and walked over to her. "Rachel, money means nothing to me. I have enough to keep Leiper's Fork functioning for a long time and I got every dollar honestly. And yes, I was pumping gas but not at the filling station." He attempted to laugh. "It's a long time dream come true and I've been blessed beyond what I deserve."

As he towered above her and lifted his hands in exasperation, she cowered and covered her head. The thought of another man with his arms in the air made Rachel cry out.

"No, Jesse! Please don't hit me. Please don't." She pleaded with pain filled eyes then prepared to receive his blows. Jesse stood back in horror, as Rachel whimpered and rocked her body slowly.

"Honey! Rachel, honey! What are you saying? I would never hit you. I'd rather hold you, princess. What made you think, I would ever hit the woman I love?"

Rachel's voice was so low, he had to get on his knees to hear her. "Jesse, when you looked at me like that, I could only see Carter. He hit me with his fists that night. Hit me, where no one would see the bruises."

Jesse's nostrils flared and his eyes blazed, as he looked at her. "How dare he! How dare that animal hit you! It's a good thing he is gone, Rachel, because we'd press charges so fast his head would swim. Honey, don't ever be afraid of me. I may get angry but I will never hurt you. Do you believe me?" Rachel nodded and surrendered when he cradled her in his arms.

Jesse's eyes burned. "I am sorry for leaving you alone with him. And I'm sorry I cannot tell you everything Rachel, but I can't. Trust me, honey. One day, it will all make sense. Now, I can tell you this. I did ask Tony to hire you. You are an outstanding artist and what artist from New York knows about this wonderful town? I wanted you here, and after he saw your work, he did too. Remember, Tony Hunter is an artist in his own right and a darn good one. He thinks you did a superb job and so do I. Almost every artist worth their salt receives an advance. It helps to purchase supplies and if nothing else, gets them off to a good start so they don't have to worry about making ends meet while they are working. I thought you knew that, but evidently you didn't." Jesse ran a hand across his face. "I probably need to go now, Rachel. I'm bushed and I think you've had enough excitement for one day. I'm afraid to say anything else until I get some sleep. Never question what I say and know I love you. Hopefully, one day soon it will all make sense. However, I hope in the process, you don't give up on me. Lock your door when I leave." He stepped into the dark silence feeling more alone than ever.

Return to Leiper's Fork

Chapter 16: Gold Coins

The next morning, Jesse apologized to Mrs. Locke and spent time with her husband. As they sat near the woodpile, Mr. Locke took off his hat and rubbed his brow. "Son, I believe with all my heart my daughter loves you, but Rachel Lea has a stubborn streak just like her momma. She's as independent as can be, but I never saw a woman pine for somebody like I've seen her pine for you."

Jesse flinched. Did Rachel really love him? He hoped so.

A few brown leaves slowly drifted toward the ground in the cool morning. The air was filled with the pungent smell of fall and frost had covered everything the night before. Bill took a sip from his mug and wiped his mouth with a handkerchief from his back pocket. Jesse sat on a stump at the back of the small house, holding his steaming cup as Bill picked up a piece of wood, took out his pocket knife and without another word started whittling. Jesse watched quietly, wondering what to say. He wanted to pour out his heart to the man who had befriended him _ the man he loved. Moments passed and Bill Locke continued to whittle. Leiper's Fork knew Bill Locke as an expert carver. His collection of carved figures was for sale at Leiper's Fork Art Gallery and The Barn.

During the silence, without missing a beat between his blade and the piece of wood he was carving, Bill Locke's eyes shifted toward Jesse. "She could have had dates, you know. One time, that Tony was coming for supper but at the last minute it didn't work out. Don't know if it was him or her. Some rich dude came in from Dallas. Seems he saw her work there in Nashville. He tried every trick in the book to get her to go to work for him at the Dallas Fort-Worth Airport but Rachel Lea told him she wasn't leaving Leiper's Fork. Seems with all the changes going on there and the construction, he wanted her to paint some of the history of Texas on the walls like she's been doing here. He took her to dinner and wined and dined her for two days. Even bought her an expensive watch but she told him there was no way she was leaving for four months. "I believe he would

have married her if she'd been willing. He even told her she looked better than them Dallas Cowboy cheerleaders." Jesse grunted, as Bill chortled.
"Gave him back that watch he gave her, too. Don't think he was too happy when she did that. He roared out of here like a bat out of Mammoth Cave. My girl ain't moved by money."

Jesse laughed. Rachel sure had spunk and he knew she wouldn't move anywhere for long. He could see the little spit fire handing the watch back to the Texas dude. Nobody could ever buy Rachel Benton and he'd never tried regardless of what she thought. Money didn't move him either.

Bill's eyes shot up and he gave Jesse a searching look before continuing.
"The girl has all kinds of chances to go places and do stuff but she's a hometown girl and no amount of money is going to make her change her mind. She never said another word about it after he left. Rachel goes to church, eats, sleeps and works with her flowers. She even created a line of jeweled pumpkins and sold them in the gift shops here, in Franklin and in Nashville. They're just the prettiest little things you ever did see. Those pumpkin stalks are hand made in her studio and she covers those silk and velvet pumpkins with pearls and diamonds and all kinds of stuff. My favorite was the one with the silver hummingbird nest on the side. She's quite a young woman you know."

Quite the woman and I can't seem to get to first base with her. Rachel, will you ever believe I love you?

Bill took a drink of his coffee, wiping his mouth with his sleeve. "She's always looking for something to make. She loves you, son. I didn't get any schooling past twelfth grade but I'm smart enough to know what makes my girl happy. If she ever wakes up and wants you to be a part of her life, you have my blessings. You sure do." Bill averted his eyes to the shape he was whittling. Showing emotion was one thing he didn't intend to do. He'd always kept his emotions in check and to show them publicly was one thing he never did. The woodshed was where he went and he could count those trips on one hand. The last time he'd cried was when his wife had lost their baby boy to a miscarriage. If he'd been spared, Bill Locke Jr. would be five years younger than Jesse. As he looked at the face of the man sitting near him, Bill knew that sooner or later, he'd have to make a trip to the woodshed. He'd never seen such a sad face on a man in his life.

Jesse called Bill's name and a pair of faded blue eyes turned toward him.

Return to Leiper's Fork

"Bill, you've known me all my life. If I had serious character flaws, you'd know them by now. I'm not perfect but if I love somebody, I don't keep it a secret. I love God, your daughter, and Leiper's Fork in that order. When my grandfather married my grandmother, he gave her one hundred Gold Eagle, twenty-five dollar coins. When Dad married Mom, he gave them to her. I'm reminded of Abraham sending his servant to find a wife for his son, Isaac. Rebecca offered to water his camels and put him up for the night in her family's tent. The servant gave her gifts of gold and took her away the next day." Jesse reached into his jacket pocket and pulled out a faded velvet bag. "These gold coins have been in the safe for thirty years. Mom told me when she got mad at dad, she'd open the safe and the coins would remind her of how much he loved her. I'm not sure exactly what one of these is worth but I want you to keep them for Rachel." The older man's mouth opened to object but Jesse stopped him.

"When the time is right, tell her they are from me. By the way, Susanna never saw these coins. I couldn't give them to a woman I didn't love. Those are for Rachel. I made a big mistake years ago Bill, and there's not a day goes by, I don't remember that. I may have lost her forever but by God's grace and mercy, I pray I might get another chance." Jesse pointed to the faded bag in Bill's hand. "Keep them for her."

"Now wait, son. I know you love my girl and I think Rachel Lea will come around one of these here days. You don't need to ask permission from me to marry her. You two are grown adults now. You do whatever you want. Now, as far as this bag of gold coins, you're talking money. Lots of money." Bill fingered the crimson velvet with his rough, chapped hands.

"Son, you better keep this in your safe." Jesse backed off, as Bill tried to place them in his hand.

"No, Bill. I want to do things right and I want your blessings. If Rachel is not in the mood to accept them, you keep them. She is the only woman I've ever wanted to marry. The money means nothing to me anymore. Now, I am leaving for Houston but I need your help in a couple of weeks." For a few more minutes the two men put their heads together and talked quietly. Before Jesse left, Bill wrapped his long, strong arms around the younger man.

"Son, it's all going to work out. As sure as there is a God in Heaven, it will work out alright. My girl's eyes will open, sooner or later. I'll do my best to help you." Bill gave Jesse a handshake. "Are you going to see Rachel before you leave?"

"I don't think so, Bill. She's not too happy with me now. She needs her space and she needs to work through a few things. I could go over there but it might make things worse. She thinks I love money more than her but you know the truth. At least I feel better telling you everything. Hopefully, she will see the truth in time." Bill handed the whittled shape to Jesse and Jesse could not believe what he saw. Bill Locke had carved the likeness of his daughter wearing a wedding gown. As Jesse held the wooden object in his hands, he hoped one day, to hold her as his bride.

The older man shaded his eyes as the trail of dust from Jesse's car loomed in the distance. "I never got to raise my son but I've got one now, and it sure feels good." Bill Locke headed for the back door but on second thought, followed the path to the woodshed.

As Jesse drove down the highway toward the airport, he knew he not only loved Rachel but Bill and Lorene Locke and he knew they loved him. He brushed away the tears and glanced at the wooden figure in the seat next to him.

Guess Bill's about fifty by now. I remember Rachel saying her parents thought they would never be blessed with children. Then God gave them a wonderful daughter and I want her for my wife. I'll do whatever it takes to win her.

As the jet left BNA that Saturday morning, Jesse gazed out the window wishing he could see Leiper's Fork. The only thing he saw, as the plane ascended were thousands of buildings, numerous patches of trees, the dark winding Cumberland River and tiny black ribbons of highway. December was on the horizon and the land was ready for a winter's rest. He thought of Rachel far below and wondered what she was doing. He thought she could still be sleeping soundly in her cozy bed but maybe she was up early, capturing something on her canvass. He remembered battling with himself about calling her, before he boarded the plane. He'd have to trust God to work out the details. He'd heard for years that absence made the heart grow fonder but he wasn't sure in this case. He hoped so. In early December, he'd return to Leiper's Fork for the Christmas Parade. He'd been asked to be the Grand Marshall and later he would dedicate Leiper's Fork Museum and Gardens to the town. He wasn't sure how Rachel would react or if she

Return to Leiper's Fork

would even see him again. Would Bill Locke come to his rescue?

Jesse prayed, as talk buzzed all around him. Already, the jet was far above the gray, somber November clouds headed toward Seattle at thirty-five thousand feet. As he looked up, the petite attendant with dark brown hair and pert green eyes was studying him. He smiled quickly, averting his eyes to the window. She was the same attendant who had been overly friendly with him on his trip down. He guessed, she'd had a layover in Nashville over the holidays and was on the return trip to Seattle. The attendant continued gazing in his direction, enjoying the sight of the man in a navy sweater and jeans. Realizing temptation was at his door, Jesse pulled out his Nook. He'd read a book as long as he could stay awake. Coffee would soon be served but before he knew it, his head was nodding. The observant attendant decided to write her phone number on his napkin, when she served snacks later. Some minutes later, Jesse jerked his head and saw a pair of sea green eyes peering down at him. "Sir, would you like to have something to drink?" She laid a napkin on his tray.

A knock on the door brought Rachel out of her doldrums. Since early that morning, she had lingered in her rocking chair, watching the sun come up and sipping coffee. Most of all, she had prayed. She needed direction and that direction and wisdom could only come from one source _ God.

Lord, have you sent help this fast?

Bill looked into the sleepy brown eyes of his daughter and saw the dark circles under them. He knew she had not slept well the night before." I've got something to say and I want you to listen well. Daughter, if you love Jesse, consider him sent by God. Randall cannot return and I know you loved him but you can't spend your life grieving for someone who is dead. And don't say you're not, because your daddy knows you better than that. Randall would not want to come back to this old sinful world after he's tasted the beauty and wonders of Heaven."

Rachel started to speak but Bill hushed her. "Now, Rachel Lea, you know that's true, so you've got to go on with your life. God set the calendar for his birth and for his going home and there's nothing you can do about it because that's God's business. He had a plan for Randall and he has a plan for you. Girl, you've got to go on living and I think part of that plan includes Jesse Steed. There ain't no better man in Williamson County. At least that's what I think."

Rachel placed her hands on her hips and slowly exhaled. "Now, Dad! Don't interfere when you've not been invited and I mean it. I don't interfere every time you and Mom have an argument and don't you try to interfere in my love life or lack of one. Your daughter is a grown woman in case you forgot. I respect your opinions but don't . . .just don't, Dad. "

"Rachel, sometimes I think dads don't interfere when maybe they should. Jesse Steed is a fine Christian man. He sure comes from good stock and he's got a mansion for you to live in. That's saying a lot these days for a girl who's been raised in a poor family like ours. All my life, I've wanted to give your momma things but I've never been able to give her a mansion. She knows I love her and that's the important thing, as far as we're concerned. When I was real sick, she pulled me through and took in some work, so we could pay the doctor bills." He hesitated. "You didn't know this but when I asked her to marry me, she turned me down. Said she wasn't sure if I could afford to get married. She could have married some guy who had a whole lot more than me but she knew I loved her and would provide the best I could for her. The best thing I know is that when the day is over, I get to go home to a woman who loves me, even if we've had a disagreement that morning. Sometimes, things are about as clear as mud between us but love covers a multitude of mistakes and I'm sure I've been the cause of many of them. Sometimes, we don't understand what the other is going through and we think we've been mistreated, because of what they said or did. It's easy to get mad but it's not easy to say you're sorry and ask forgiveness. I can tell you, that Jesse loves you and you hold that man's heart in your hand . . . at least for a while." Bill's eyes flickered as they met Rachel's. He looked away when he saw her tearing up. "You know daughter, sometimes a man might get tired of waiting when a woman can't make up her mind or if she wants to live in the past. I'd hate to see something come between you and Jesse. Now he's got a lot of irons in the fire and he can't tell you everything, so you're going to live by faith for a while. That's what marriage is about. Now, look at this."

Bill pulled a small bag from his thick jacket. A plunking noise followed as he set it on the table. "I've thought and thought what to do about this and Lorene and me figured this was the best plan. This bag has one hundred American Gold Eagle twenty-five dollar coins in it. Jesse told me to give it to you. That boy beats all I've ever seen. I tried to get him to take

Return to Leiper's Fork

it back and he said it was your gift. Kind of like Rebecca's when Abraham sent his servant to find a wife for Isaac. She left with him the next day to become his bride and, no, she didn't have a lot of questions about her husband. She didn't know what kind of man he was or what he did for a living. She had no idea what he even looked like. Girl, that's faith and love. She knew he loved her, because, you see daughter, he trusted his father to find the right woman for him. You see God had already picked her out but he had to lead the servant to her. Isaac sent gifts ahead, and God blessed him with a beautiful woman. I think you are the woman God intended for Jesse. See daughter, he has already sent this wedding gift ahead for you. I guess you could say, your dad is the servant. Anyway, I think he's waiting for you and praying you'll make the right decision. I've already given him my blessings, in case he asks for your hand in marriage."

Dad!" Rachel threw herself in her father's arms and he held her as she sobbed. "I've been praying about my hard heart for hours and I do love Jesse. I just don't understand what all of the secrets are about. As Rachel rested her head against her father's rock hard chest, Bill Locke soothed her with words only a father can say to his daughter.

"Rachel Lea, Jesse loves you. He has trusted our Father to find his bride and he sent his wedding gift ahead. He's waiting for you to make up your mind. You don't know the story but Jesse told me, that his granddaddy gave these coins to his bride on their wedding day. Then, when Jesse's daddy got married, he gave them to his bride. When she got mad at him she went to the safe and looked at those coins. She knew he loved her very much. Forgiveness, love and trust are needed before and after marriage."

Rachel looked at the bag of coins. "Dad, I'm not sure. I've been hurt but maybe I need to do some forgiving. I didn't know what was going on and I thought Jesse felt sorry for me. I know better, now." She kissed her father. "Thanks Dad. You are the best."

Bill Locke tweaked his daughter's chin. "I don't know what the future will bring for you two, but I'll have Lorene send my best suit to the cleaners, just in case. Might just have to buy me one of them new gold designer ties from, The Barn." After wiping his brow with his faded bandanna, Bill Locke drove slowly down the lane. Being a dad wasn't easy but the toughest day ahead for him would be the day he'd walk his only child down the aisle. At least he hoped so.

Rachel fingered the faded, velvet bag. Releasing the ties, she peered inside. Reverently, she poured the coins on the table. Their clinking sound reminded her of the night Jesse left. She could still hear the door close. She had been so angry, she refused to tell him goodbye. Counting the coins one by one, she made ten stacks. "My goodness! With the price of gold these days . . ." She mentally calculated the price of the coins. "Seventeen hundred dollars for each coin! Jesse, have you lost your mind? After all I've said and done, you want to marry me. Your heart is good but mine is black. Please forgive me."

That night, Rachel searched her Bible, until she found the story of Isaac and Rebecca. "He loved her so much he was waiting in the fields for her. Jesse, you don't have any camels for me to water but I will accept your gift and wait for you. I have my answer, already."

Return to Leiper's Fork

Chapter 17: Christmas Parade

Jesse watched as freighter after freighter entered the Gulf of Mexico and neared their destination_ Houston Oil Refinery. After weeks at sea, the freighters filled with oil had journeyed down the Pacific coasts, where the crude oil would be refined and sent across the nation. Jesse had overseen delivery into the freighters as they filled with oil from the oil sands in Canada. From there, he had flown to Houston to oversee the unloading.

Years of debating the issue of Canadian Oil had come to a close. Whether it was by pipeline to the United States or by rail or ship, the oil was coming. In Jesse's case, it was by ship. Jesse remembered the debate had been fierce and his company, JHR Oil Corporation was the first to extract the oil and export it to the United States.

Environmentalists tried to persuade the government the project would be destructive to the boreal forest that set on top of the tarry rock, from which the oil was extracted but Jesse had spoken before Congress and won them over. He had challenged the opponents with facts from himself and experts representing the different arenas of the debate. He stood before congressmen and the Secretary of the Interior. As he spoke, he remembered it took only one stone to take down Goliath and he had a pocket full. "Oil sands extraction is getting cleaner and represents a potentially major source of oil from a politically stable ally. The stakes are enormous. The oil sands have reserves of 171.3 billion barrels, according to estimates by the government of Alberta. This is enough to change the balance of world oil markets. It is time the United States quits being held hostage by a few nations in the world and especially one who wants to halt ships in the Strait of Hormuz. This oil will ensure America's energy security and we have the refineries in place to handle the thick crude."

Thunderous applause followed Jesse's speech. As some congressmen cheered, a few shook their head in frustration. The majority of congress was tired of the high prices. Supporters of the oil filled the halls and marched in the streets of Washington. The price of gas had crippled the American economy and Americans were tired of being held hostage by heads of state, controlling the production and price of oil. Voters were sending messages if something wasn't done, they were cleaning house next election. Jesse remembered that day, as he and other proponents defended the right to import the Canadian oil. His uncles had stood with him and acted downright giddy, after Congress voted to approve the measure.

Uncle Herb hugged him. "Son, if you father had heard you speak, he would have been proud of you. See his dream is coming true. When we were boys, we heard tales from the folks in Canada, there was oil under that ground. We were up there vacationing with your grandfather, who was a sharp business man. We were just kids but Dad had a vision. Dad leased the ground and had a geologist take core samples. He knew we had a good thing. This has taken years, but we've put every dime we had into leasing more land. Then we formed the corporation. At one time, your daddy was ready to sell his blue Cadillac but Virginia talked him out of it. Said it was the most comfortable car she'd ever been in. Clyde would be proud today. It's been worth every sacrifice we made." Uncle Herb wiped his brow and his eyes, as his brother Ron, looked on. He swept back his thick gray hair with one hand and stroked his moustache with the other. In his slow southern accent he continued. "Dad said if we ever wanted anything, we'd better work for it and we certainly did. Tonight, we're going to eat a steak in his honor. In fact, I'm ready for a large T-bone right now." Jesse smiled. Today, a victory had been won. A dream had come true. He only hoped the dream he'd had for a lifetime would bring him the happiness he'd always wanted.

As he filled out paperwork in the refinery's office, his cell rang. He saw at once it was Tony Hunter. "Jesse, Rachel's work is finished. Do you want me to find her something else to do? The murals are quite striking and you made a great decision when you recommended her. I hope she makes it for the dedication. She wasn't sure if she wanted to be acknowledged."

"Tony, that sounds good. Tell Rachel, she is expected the day of dedication. If she doesn't abide by her contract, the corporation can sue her for half of her salary. That should wake her from a sound sleep. Don't know if she read it or not but bring it to her attention. The money isn't the issue but she needs to be there. In fact she must be there." Jesse cleared his throat.

Return to Leiper's Fork

"Now, for the big news! Eight freighters just arrived with the Canadian oil. This is the first shipment with more to come, so I'm leaving for Seattle very soon. I've got a zillion papers to fill out. Don't worry about Rachel. We only have two weeks until the Christmas Parade and I'm not missing it, if we have fifty freighters in port. By the way, I'm bringing a special young woman with me and I think you know her. She can't wait to see Leiper's Fork and I'm doing everything I can, to make sure she makes it her home. I've even offered her a job to work with you. I just might tell you she is tickled pink. Quite a doll, that Lydia. Know I'm returning with a blond beauty on my arm and she's counting the days until she says, 'I do.' Sure glad I found her. By the way Tony, I'm glad you turned down Rachel's invitation to dinner. You don't deserve her." Jesse laughed and placed his cell in his pocket after Tony threatened to get even with him.

Rachel, it's been difficult without seeing you. I've decided to accompany Lydia home and I hope you understand.

Two weeks later, a weary Jesse and Lydia carried their suitcases to the rented car. They had been traveling since five that morning. In less than an hour, the Christmas Parade would start. Perspiration popped out on Jesse's forehead, as he traveled faster than the speed limit allowed. Lydia slept and as Jesse glanced at her, he saw how truly beautiful she was _ the type every man wants to marry. Her long golden hair formed a halo around her oval shaped face and her dark fringed lashes rested on pink cheeks. Lydia was a perfect specimen of womanhood and he was glad he found her.

Lydia, if I had found you months ago, I wouldn't have agonized so much. You are going to make my life so much simpler and you're going to be so happy. I knew you had to be the woman I needed, when I first saw you.

Lydia's two piece suit fit her body to perfection and she glowed with an innocence that shook Jesse to his very core. He remembered the long looks and admiring glances, men had given her when they entered the airport. Even some of the young soldiers had whistled from a distance and turned for second looks. After speeding down Old Franklin Road for some time, he neared Leiper's Fork. The large historical marker at the town's edge greeted him. He decided to shake the sleeping woman. "Lydia, wake up, honey. We're here. I thought you might want to freshen your make up before you get out of the car." Reaching over, he pushed back a strand of her golden blond hair. Jesse was proud to be bringing such a beautiful woman to Leiper's Fork but how would Rachel react when she saw them together? Jesse stroked his jaw and groaned.

Awake, after a long nap, Lydia pulled herself up and grabbed Jesse's hand. "Jesse, you have made my dream complete. The next best thing that can happen to me is to marry the man I love. I can hardly wait to return to Seattle for the wedding." She smiled the smile of a woman in love and gave Jesse a kiss on the cheek.

Crowds were heavy that afternoon, as Jesse quickly parked his rental and hurried Lydia through the throngs of people waiting along Old Hillsboro Road. He wanted to stop and talk but he had to locate Tony, who said he'd be watching for him. As he looked around, he saw a blushing Tony hurrying through the crowd toward them. Lydia reached out to hug the excited man.

"The little blond can ride with you today, can't she? I've got to escort Rachel." Jesse quickly shook Tony's hand and pointed to a line of cars.

"I'm at your service, Jesse, especially when there's a beautiful woman to rescue." Hurriedly, Jesse ran to a shiny, blue car parked behind Barney Fife's police car. Bill Locke stood at the back of the car and shook Jesse's hand.

"I was getting a bit nervous, son. Sure glad you made it." Jesse glanced inside to see Rachel peering in the mirror.

With his heart racing, he opened the car door and jumped inside. Already, a man was speaking over the megaphone and the black and white police car's engine was humming. As Jesse turned toward his passenger, to give her a hug, the woman beside him shrieked and flung her lipstick in the air.

"What are you doing in my car?" Rachel blushed and pointed to Jesse, as if he had been an armed intruder. She fanned her face with one hand and gasped for air. Jesse watched not believing how Rachel was acting. He had done nothing to cause her anger.

Calmly, he responded. "The question I believe has been asked by the

Return to Leiper's Fork

wrong person, Miss Benton. I think I should have asked you why you are in my car. As Jesse cocked an eyebrow, Rachel gritted her teeth then faced him with a fierceness he'd never seen.

"Jesse Steed! I was minding my own business and waiting for Dad to chauffer me in the parade, when you jumped in to purposely irritate me. My father is going to be very upset when he sees you have taken his place. By the way, that was very rude of you to pawn that woman off on Tony. He's not here to babysit your par . . . paramour or whatever you want to call her. I saw you when you drove up. She was clinging to you like a tick to a coon dog." Rachel spat out her words knowing she could never trust Jesse Steed if he wore wings and a halo. Bitterly, she added, "Dad is supposed to be driving me today! How do you think you've made him feel?"

So I've provoked Rachel Benton to jealousy and that's what this is all about. That's a good thing even though it's been a long time coming but Lydia is not what she thinks.

In his most charming voice, he quipped, "Miss Benton, I believe the sign states, I am the Grand Marshall and not Bill Locke, even though he's a very fine man."

"You're Grand Marshall over my dead body, Jesse!" Rachel slumped in the seat, after reaching for her purse. "I don't think I can stay in this car with you. I feel like a hostage." Scowling, she looked away. She was thoroughly disgusted with him and Jesse knew it.

"Rachel, it's a little late to start frowning and scowling, so paste on a smile. You've got a crowd to please. Look happy for once." As his jaw tightened, he gave his tie a jerk and pressed his lips together in determination.

What did I read last night in the Book of James about being glad for tribulation?

He studied the elegant curve of her neck and breathed in her perfume as she in turn studied the dashboard and sniffed the fresh leather scent invading the Cadillac. "You know, I wanted you to be my girl at prom but you made plans with someone else. But that's water under the bridge now, isn't it?" Jesse could not forget wishing Rachel had been with him in his car rather than Susanna. Hearing no reply, he continued. "I've got air-conditioning, dimmer, radio, leather seats and a three ninety engine not to mention white walls, and fender skirts." He looked in her direction hoping for some type of response.

Rachel ignored him and scowled deeply. She guessed he had to say something but he didn't need to brag about the car he was driving. She decided to file her nails while Jesse talked about his car. He patted her hand.

"I need to warn you about something. I've also got electric seats and electric doors. So smile, because I'm not letting you out until you do." He directed his attention to the crowd and waved while Rachel fumed and attempted a smile. Jesse Steed was not a man she wanted to reckon with, much less fight but how did it happen that he was always right and she was always wrong? As a battle raged within her, Jesse reached across the wide seat. "I'm sorry you are angry with me but I wanted to tell you something that's more important than this car. You didn't need to check your makeup, Rachel. I've never seen you more beautiful. For what it's worth, these last weeks have been too long. I missed you, honey." He searched her face hoping for some understanding but Rachel's eyes had turned to ice. The pain was so great it was as if Jesse's heart was splintering into a thousand fragments.

Without hesitating, she spat out her venom. "Oh! Men! I wouldn't trust one as far as I could throw them." As she spoke, she knew she had to get control of her feelings. People had come to enjoy the parade and she'd been mad all morning. But why take it out on the crowd? At that moment, she wanted to cry but she wouldn't give Jesse the pleasure of seeing her break down. Jesse had rejected her for someone else no matter what he'd said the last time he had seen her or what he'd said minutes ago about missing her. Rachel could only blame herself. After the parade he would rescue his beautiful blonde from Tony and she would be alone.

The Master of Ceremonies, with megaphone in hand, reminded the crowd to get on one side of the road or the other because the parade was ready to start. With exuberance, he shouted, "Welcome to the Leiper's Fork Christmas Parade! There's nothing like it in the United States or the world. You see, it's unique and one of a kind. Kind of country and homemade like many of us here today. If you're from Leiper's Fork, that means you're special, even if we're a bit slow paced. Soon our Grand Marshall, Mr. Jesse Steed, will start the engine of his "61" Cadillac de Ville and accompanying him will be one of our artists, Miss Rachel Benton."

Return to Leiper's Fork

Jesse grunted in agreement. "Harold, you're right for once. She is sitting by my side, madder than an old wet hen but she's with me." Jesse started the engine and the Cadillac slowly moved forward. The sound reminded him of a kitten's purr. He clicked the door again for good measure and cleared his throat while Rachel sat refusing to acknowledge his presence.

Finally, she pointed to an old truck beside one of the buildings and whispered hoarsely, "I would trade this car for the rusted truck, over there, if you'd open my door."

Slowly they moved down Old Hillsboro Road behind Leiper's Fork law enforcement. The black and white police car, a proud symbol of the village was a welcome sight to everyone. The driver raced his engine and as the car backfired, Rachel screamed. The crowd roared with laughter. "Do it again!" The exuberant children shouted.

Jesse reached over to grab Rachel's hand. "Honey, it's okay. Just a little noise from the police car. Relax, sweetheart." He continued to grip her trembling hand as she fanned her face. She looked at him. When he turned on the charm, the effects were devastating. How much more handsome could one man get? "Are you going to be okay?" Rachel ignored him for a moment. Regardless of how her heart felt, she wanted to hurt him. Had he not hurt her, when he came driving up with a beautiful blond?

"You're wearing a mighty expensive suit, you know. Aren't you overdressed for the occasion? You only had to escort me in the parade, not stand up and give a speech to the country. By the way, whose car did you borrow, Jesse?" A frozen smile formed on her lips, as she studied the man who seemed totally unoffended. Jesse thought he wouldn't trade this day with Rachel for a million barrels of oil. She was finally coming around, even if she was angry. Had the little, petite blond from Seattle stirred Rachel? He prayed things would work out in his favor.

Jesse's response was slow and deliberate. "Whose car did I borrow, Rachel? The only answer I have is this. The Cadillac belongs to me. It used to be my dad's and I inherited it after his death. You see, he owned a dealership in Nashville and one day he drove this two door, "61" Cadillac de Ville, home. After that he was sold on the Dresden Blue. It's been in the garage for quite a number of years but I recently had it restored. Clay, a friend of mine from Missouri, did the work and he is the best around. Even drives one just like it. Notice the real leather, Rachel. Top of the line! Only a handful of Dresden Blues were ever made and Clay and I own one." Jesse stroked the fine blue leather as if it was worth a million dollars.

"That's why I kept her. Long, lean, beautiful, great shape and I'd give her a perfect ten. Some baby my car." Jesse kissed his finger and touched the dashboard. Rachel fumed silently as Jesse secretly smiled. She was held behind locked doors. Her captor was none other than the well dressed, wealthy and very handsome Jesse Steed and Jesse always got what he wanted. She forced a smile and decided to have the time of her life. A little jealousy might make him mad but she would pay him back for the trouble he had caused her. It didn't matter if Jesse had brought that woman with him. She would forget him or die trying and if he loved her, his anger would show.

Some of the soldiers dared a handsome dark haired army captain to throw her a kiss. Rachel in turn smiled and threw one back. "I'll see you later, gorgeous!" He pointed to Rachel who responded gushingly. "I can't wait, soldier." Jesse pretended to not hear but could not ignore the jealousy brewing inside him. A muscle twitched in his jaw, as he forced a smile to his lips. Would everything back fire today or worse, would he lose Rachel in the process?

Jesse turned the corner and parked his car behind the church. Sighing, he looked at her. "Come on beautiful. Let's walk up and watch the rest of the parade." He gazed at her but she ignored him.

How dare Jesse act as if he's done nothing! He'd better find his girlfriend. I don't know how I'll make him pay for the way he has treated me but I'll think of something.

Rachel spewed forth poison like volcanoes spew forth deadly ashes.

"Unlock my door right now, Jesse! I've had all I can take. You said you loved me and I waited for you. Then you come home bringing a woman you've had with you, God only knows how long. I feel like such a fool. Go find your blond beauty and get lost! I hope I never see you again." After hearing a click, she pushed the door and stumbled blindly through the crowd. Jesse sat stunned before unfolding himself from the car.

"Wait, Rachel! It's not what you think, sweetheart. You're mistaken." Jesse's words faded in the noise of the crowd. His eyes blazed with anger

Return to Leiper's Fork

and disappointment. He tried to follow her but she quickly disappeared from sight. He stood alone, searching with his eyes, not realizing Rachel was only a short distance away. She watched as Jesse put on his designer glasses and scanned the crowd. She wondered what he meant earlier when he said she was mistaken. Mistaken about what? As he turned away, she saw disappointment on his face. With bent shoulders, he walked alone in the direction of his car.

Jesse, I love you but you don't love me. Right now, I am so angry with how I've been treated I don't know what to do. I will be at the dedication but it will take everything I've got to attend. All I want is to leave town for a long time and get my broken heart healed. I can't stand to see you in love with that gorgeous woman. She's perfect in every way and I'm not. I can't bear to lose you but it is too late.

Soon, the local Boy Scout Troop led in the Pledge of Allegiance and the national anthem. The Master of Ceremonies followed by announcing the names and ranks of soldiers marching proudly behind the American flag, held high by an aged veteran. Proud soldiers nodded to the crowd and waved to those who boldly called out, "We're proud of you, young people! Welcome home, heroes." Fathers hoisted toddlers on their shoulders and mothers held babes in their arms. Young boys and girls saluted to the brave men and women who fought to defend their nation. This was a proud day in Leiper's Fork. Home town heroes were being honored. A high school student on a flatbed truck boldly sang, *God Bless America*, as sentimental bystanders hummed the tune.

Jesse bowed his head and leaned against his car. His efforts to win Rachel had back fired, as had Barney Fife's police car. He had failed to win her love. Rachel turned away after watching him for some time.

Jesse, I do care but right now, I am hurting like never before.

The crowd laughed and cheered as politicians in long black cars, smiled and shouted. One dropped the sign he was holding and had to stop his car to get out and pick it up. Well trained horses of many different breeds pranced and trotted to the crowd's delight and a truck filled with squealing baby pigs, delighted children and adults alike.

A flock of sheep wearing brown felt reindeer antlers was led by a shepherd and was followed by a bright red fire truck. As it inched down the road, the fun loving firefighter decided to set off the piercing siren. The young people laughed and shrieked, as the elderly put their hands to their ears. Frightened sheep trotted into the middle of the crowd, followed by the shepherd who was frantically trying to control them.

After that, young dancers wearing pink lipstick and rouge whirled and strutted in brightly colored costumes. They were proud to show off their latest dance steps to friends and family. Soon followed the waste disposal truck, with an exuberant driver who waved and cheered to the crowd. A wagon of cheerleaders followed pitching candy to excited children.

The football team followed and proudly held the trophy they had won. Then came a lawn care truck and the high school band which proudly strutted to a popular tune. When the crowd thought the parade was over, the hero everyone had come to see, popped around the bend driving a candy apple Red Wing trike with a matching trailer. Santa boomed with laughter, as small children screamed, "Santa is here! Santa is here!" Amid their shrieks of joy, the jolly elf reminded them he would be at the Lawn Chair Theater to hear their Christmas wishes until time for everyone to leave for the museum. He began handing out candy canes as the children pressed forward to touch the man in red velvet. Two women nearby whispered about Santa's identity.

"Now, Edna, I know he's not Tom Cummings 'cause he just isn't that fat."

"Josephine, if you saw Tom eat, like I've seen him, you'd think twice. I sure do believe it is Tommy Cummins because I had that boy in my seventh grade Algebra class. Never did understand about variables and equations. Anyway, I'd know Tommy if he was dressed like a turkey. You do know he ended up teaching Kindergarten don't you?"

Edna placed her hands to her mouth and whispered, "Well, shut my mouth! It's a good thing those kindergarteners don't need to know Algebra."

As the parade wound down, Mayor Anderson reminded the crowd the dedication of the museum would occur in two hours. He encouraged them to shop the stores for all of the homemade crafts and special gifts on display for Christmas. People milled around Country Boy Restaurant, and

Return to Leiper's Fork

Puckett's Grocery and Restaurant grabbing sodas, burgers and homemade sandwiches made to order. Shoppers filed into, Yeomen's In the Fork Rare Books, for a treasure they knew would never be found in the city. Some sauntered over to Joe Natural's for a hot cup of coffee, a roast beef sandwich and a piece of fresh strawberry cake with vanilla icing. Some even grabbed a jar of Joe's prized honey collected from his own bees. Many trickled into the antique stores hoping to find a Christmas bargain at just the right price. Sweet smelling soaps and special pieces of jewelry were quickly snatched up and placed in bags and many carried sacks with the Gypsy's logo. Rachel studied the Gringo boots as two elderly women pointed to the pretty owner and examined a rack of clothing. "Yes, her husband is a TV star and she sings in a band at the Gypsy Moon Ball down at the creek in April. Can you imagine such a thing? And that's not all. I heard tell she was a registered pharmacist. Maybe I'll talk to her about my arthritis."

The other looked around. "Well, do tell. If I looked like her, maybe somebody would let me sing in their band." She batted her eyes as she glanced in the mirror attempting to smooth wrinkles on her face and neck. She pressed her thin lips together and smiled. "I sang soprano in the church choir years ago and if I say so it was lovely. We need to go. I heard tell, The Barn has a line of ties made from vintage fabrics and Barney told me to be sure and pick him one for Christmas morning. He's singing a solo, himself." Pressing her lips together one last time, she adjusted her glasses and grabbed the arm of her friend.

Rachel found herself looking at a gold bracelet in Serenite Maidon's. Her heart skipped a beat as she fingered the delicate gold charms. "So lovely."

The owner stepped over immediately. "This line of jewelry is designed especially for us. Each bracelet is twenty-two karat gold and very unique. If you'd like, we can get one especially made for you." She looked at Rachel, knowing the bracelets wouldn't last long.

There was no question in Rachel's mind they were special. "I'm trusting Santa to come down my chimney this year. If he drops by here, please tell him this is the present I want." She walked out smiling, remembering the antique lighting fixtures, apothecary cabinets and gigantic wooden clock faces, along with European pocket watches, mirrors, garden containers and all of the lovely pieces of jewelry she had seen. As she glanced back, she noticed a worn leather ottoman in the window. "Somebody will take that in a New York minute and I'm going to be mad at myself for not purchasing it for the cabin."

She stepped up to the Old Natchez House, a gallery of beautiful paintings and different works befitting a historic 1890's house and picked out a gift for Betsy, then hurried over to Laurel Leaf Gallery. She admired the art work and the many different gifts on display. Minutes later she purchased a piece of jewelry for her mother's Christmas present. Glancing at her watch, she decided to visit one more store, then hurry off to the dedication.

As she walked, she noticed some of the old timers still sitting in their rocking chairs, discussing the weather and talking about how their crops faired during the extra hot summer. Wives stood by discussing the surprise baby shower they were holding in the church basement for the pastor's wife and the desserts they were planning for Christmas dinner.

While Jesse was meeting with some of the men, who were admiring his car, he noticed Rachel leaving Serenite Maison's. He watched as the wind whipped around a building and swung her around. Caught off guard, Rachel screamed, and after noticing that people had heard her, she hurried away embarrassed. The men at Jesse's car laughed but Jesse ran toward her.

"Rachel! Rachel! Wait up!"

As the breeze continued to whip her hair, she glanced back and stepped up her pace. She had no desire to speak to the traitor. Today, should have been one of the best days of her life. She had waited six weeks to see Jesse and he had arrived with a stunning blond that stuck to him like a mosquito to fly paper. How could Jesse have treated her the way he did? Anger burned within Rachel, as she thought of how he had betrayed her. She had waited faithfully but it had proved fruitless. She laughed harshly in the wind. She'd given him the brushoff and now he was a free man. A tremor ran through her as she remembered his promise from long ago.

If you'll marry me, I'll give you Leiper's Fork and lay it at your feet.

Rachel mumbled to herself, as she entered the site. "Jesse, how I hoped when you returned, you'd say you wanted to marry me, but today our story ends. I can't marry you because you don't know the meaning of love and commitment. Marriage is sacred and love is forever. You can't continue to play the field after you say you love me." She stumbled toward the museum, hating every minute of it. In a few hours she would be home and she promised herself she'd never speak to Jesse Steed again.

Chapter 18: The Dedication

Speaking to the crowd was the hardest thing Jesse had ever done _ harder than standing before Congress in Washington, DC. He had never felt so uncomfortable in his life. He'd dressed carefully for the day, thinking a white shirt and tie, along with a new black suit would be perfect for the occasion. It didn't matter how Rachel had belittled him. What mattered is that he had lost her _ possibly for good. As he looked at the crowd, he thought surely everyone who lived in the state of Tennessee was attending the dedication. Every seat was filled and many stood behind those seated.

Rachel, Tony, Lydia, Williamson County councilmen, Mayor Anderson and Governor Bredesen, along with numerous celebrities and dignitaries were seated on the platform. Even Aubrey Preston, and Bruce and Marty Hunt had been invited. Rachel was seated directly behind Jesse at the amphitheater and after he was introduced, he felt her eyes boring into his back. His hands shook as he thought of how the day would end. This was the day he had created for his Rachel and the day he wanted to ask her to become his bride. How could it end so tragically?

Everything I planned was not only a gift for Leiper's Fork but for Rachel. Right now, I feel it was all for nothing but the good folk of Leiper's Fork will appreciate me, even if she doesn't.

Rachel frowned every time he looked at her. Jesse knew she was hurting but he knew he had done nothing to cause it. He was seeing his dream come true and he would finish what he started. "Thank you, Mayor Anderson, for your kind words. Friends and family, I welcome you today, to Leiper's Fork Museum and Gardens. This is a place where we can remember our history and our traditions. A place where we can remember those great people who taught us and who lived, dreamed and died here. Leiper's Fork is a place where our children can grow up and remember past traditions and look forward to their dreams coming true. This historic town that was begun two hundred years ago will still be alive and well in two hundred more years. You see, our people have a dream to preserve their past and protect our town from encroaching suburban development. We must work to keep alive our traditions and family values in order to see our

Return to Leiper's Fork

dreams blossom into reality. I especially thank those who have been involved in the Land Trust for Tennessee, which was started in 1999. Thanks to that effort, the Leiper's Fork area has the state's largest concentration of Land Trust protected family farms. Many of you answered the call to, *Don't zone it! Own it.* Leiper's Fork decided years ago, to define its future and not allow outside forces to do that for us. We are not a tourist town but we are a living breathing community of creative people, who have come to the attention of many around the world." Jesse hesitated and cleared his throat.

"Years ago, my father had a dream to create a beautiful museum, with a memorial garden, a theater, amphitheater, gold fish pond, a settler's cabin, and a barn for future generations of musicians and our community. Dad didn't live to see his dream come true but we're seeing its fruit. A museum was built so that the history of Leiper's Fork could remind generation after generation, of the brave folk who came and settled along Leiper's Creek. In a few minutes, you'll see murals on the walls of the museum, painted by our very own hometown artist, Miss Rachel Benton. Rachel, would you mind standing so everyone can see you?" Rachel forced a smile, but her heart was far from happy. In fact she had been downright miserable after seeing Jesse with Lydia. The audience cheered for the artist they had proudly named, *Painter of Murals.* Rachel felt tears streaming down her face but wasn't sure if they were caused by the enthusiastic crowd or from losing Jesse.

Jesse, what happened to us?

Jesse continued his speech. "Rachel has portrayed rugged and brave folk who weren't afraid to trek from Virginia and North Carolina to take the land they had been given and work day and night to see their dreams fulfilled. They were fierce, unafraid individuals who stood for what they believed and worked together to create a community. They knew what it would cost to take raw earth and create homes and farms and raise children in a Godly fashion. Many of you are direct descendants of the Benton, Leiper, Adams, Bond, Carl, Cummins, Davis, Dobbins, Hunter, Meadows, Parham, Southhall, and Wilkins families. After them, came the Sweeney, Inman, Locke, Lunn, Mayberry, Martin, Jones, and Burdette families." Jesse was interrupted momentarily as descendants of those families shouted and clapped. "It is because of our forefathers and our visionaries that we have this community today." He pointed to Aubrey Preston, and Bruce and

Marty Hunt, sitting behind him. "In the museum you will not only see murals but artifacts from 3 to 4,000 years ago. We have a fine collection of arrowheads, pottery, dishware, tools, guns, furniture, clothing, medicines, and everything that pertained to daily life. I have dedicated that museum to my parents, Clyde Austin and Virginia O'Dell Steed. Inside the museum, you will find a one room cabin, showing how a family lived on a daily basis after they got here. We have a state of the art theater, with light and sound that will give you the history of Leiper's Fork. The people look real but they are only holograms _ 3-D images projected on a 2-D surface. Watch them appear and fade away. Don't be frightened when lightning appears above your head or you feel the vibrations from hunter's guns or the growl of a bear in the wood. No one will be struck by lightning or eaten by a bear." He turned to Rachel and smiled, remembering the yard sales they attended and her fear of bears. She met his gaze without a smile. Jesse raised his eyebrows and turned back to the smiling crowd.

"The large red barn is dedicated to the youth of this area, who love to sing and play their instruments. Numerous bands of all ages have been drawn here and some of our celebrities have coached and encouraged our youth." He pointed to Aubrey Preston seated to his left. "Isn't that right, Aubrey Preston?" Aubrey nodded and gave him a thumb's up signal. "How about you, Gene Cotton? And you, Gary Hedden? Thanks for teaching your skills in recording and sound to our youth." The crowd cheered wildly as the men stood up and saluted the crowd. Gene shouted, "It's a pleasure Jesse and we're not finished yet!"

"And far from it." yelled Gary.

Everyone around Leiper's Fork knew about their efforts and those of others, in creating the Kids On Stage Foundation. From their efforts quality instruction in music, theater and visual arts had been offered to students. Jesse pointed to teens standing near him. "Every kid is somebody in Leiper's Fork and we don't believe in minuses here _ only pluses." The crowd exploded again with cheers, whistles and shrieks. Finally, Jesse raised his hand for silence. "All I ask is that you show the world what you can do and believe in yourself. The DNA of your ancestors is in your genes. They brought their music from the hills of Virginia and North Carolina. It's some of the best music in the world, in fact there's none like it. Create yours for the world out there and make us proud. Leiper's Fork is behind you all the way."

Rachel blinked back tears.

Return to Leiper's Fork

The man has the biggest heart I have ever seen. What a wonderful father he will be, someday.

Jesse continued. "We are seated in the amphitheater which will welcome a lot of entertainment. You will also see water flowing from a rock formation, over a tall limestone wall and emptying into a large pool. It then forms a winding stream beneath a walking bridge. Gold fish will live in the water all year long. Please notice, that flanking the pool is a large flat stone patio. What a beautiful place for a wedding!" Again, he glanced at Rachel, but she refused to meet his eyes. He saw her tears and wondered why she was crying.

Jesse, how can you say things like that? I suppose you're planning to be married by the pool.

Rachel bent her head, as Jesse continued to speak. "We also have a craft center. Our children can learn the crafts of their ancestors; the basket making, quilting, weaving, pottery, candle and soap making, among many other things. We also have a one room school house which was brought in from nearby. It will be open daily for meetings and educational purposes. You'll find a gift shop inside the museum that contains books about our area and many other wonderful treasures to take home. Last, but certainly not least, is an area that will touch the hearts of those who know and remember this gentleman. We have developed the Benton Memorial Gardens." Jesse gave Rachel a fleeting glance before turning back to the podium. He had remembered Randall Benton _ the man who had been his rival. As Jesse's words registered, Rachel's heart melted. She grasped Tony's hand.

"Are you okay?" he whispered.

With stricken eyes, she leaned against him. "Hold my hand, Tony. I'm praying I can make it through this. It was so unexpected."

Bill Locke placed his arm around his wife and pulled her close.
"Momma, we'd better say a quick prayer for our girl. I'm not sure she's gonna make it." Lorene, tried to smile but her trembling lips told another story. Bill Locke wondered if Rachel was going to faint. He wasn't very fast

now days but he'd be up on the stage before a hummingbird could flap his wings.

"Many of you remember Randall Benton, as 'Coach.' He died a year and a half ago." Jesse tried to smile but failed. The past ten years flashed before him. Jesse cleared his throat and struggled to maintain his composure all the while swallowing a lump that seemed to grow with every second. "Randall Benton touched our lives and hearts in many ways and he will never be forgotten. You'll see a huge sundial resting in the middle of a large, premier rose collection. That sundial reminds us we must spread kindness and goodness whenever we can. Many of you, here do that on a daily basis. We must live each day to the fullest because we are not promised tomorrow. In the memorial garden, you'll find numerous varieties of climbers, hybrid teas, miniatures and those beautiful scented roses. When spring comes, you'll smell the sweet fragrance of scented geraniums, lavender and numerous shrubs, bushes and trees. These grounds have been donated to the village of Leiper's Fork and a trust has been established for their upkeep. This will not cost Williamson County one cent. Now, I need to introduce one man who has helped make this possible. Mr. Tony Hunter from Seattle has been my right arm. He will not only be the curator but, Artist in Residence. Tony has a degree in History and Art. His works are sold in Dallas, Seattle and Chicago. He will be joined by his fiancé after their wedding. He looked at Lydia as Rachel nervously gripped her hands. After the speech, the crowd cheered and clapped. Jesse Steed had truly given a gift, to Leiper's Fork and asked for nothing in return.

As the crowd slowly moved in all directions, Rachel noticed Jesse held captive by numerous dignitaries, community leaders and town folk who wanted to thank him. She watched as he looked over the crowd, apparently searching for someone. Rachel supposed he was looking for Lydia but Tony had led her toward the museum, minutes earlier. Was Lydia waiting for Jesse and would they spend the evening together? Rachel turned away knowing she would spend the evening alone. Was her name being called? She didn't hesitate to find out.

What a fool I've been! How could I have trusted Jesse Steed? He promised if I would marry him, he would lay Leiper's Fork at my feet. Well, my feet have something to say about that, Mr. Steed!

Return to Leiper's Fork

Chapter 19: The Confrontation

Arriving home, she immediately unlocked the door and sent her shoes flying into the air. Her purse flew off her shoulder and fell with a thud against the wall. As the contents scattered across the room, Rachel flung herself on the sofa and wept openly. How long she cried, she did not know, but it seemed when she could weep no more, a car slowed and turned into her drive.

"Drats! Of all times, for someone to come!" She lifted her head from the sofa and wiped her face with her hands. Quickly, she brushed her fingers through her long locks and straightened her blouse. When she reached the door, she jumped back. A tall man with dark hair was standing there but his face was turned from her. Was he the soldier she had flirted with earlier? How did he find her house? Dare she open the door to him? Her heart pounded within her. Had the man seen her? Several knocks later, he called loudly, "Rachel! Let me in." Hearing no sound in the room, he knocked again. "Rachel, I know you're home. I'm going to count to three and then you'll have to replace this door because it is not going to look the same after I get finished with it." Relief flooded her as she recognized the voice. She wiped her brow. It was Jesse but what was he doing at her house when he should have been with Lydia?

The door's not locked, if he's brave enough to come in. After all what is keeping him from doing what he wants to do. He always gets his way but if he breaks down that door, he just might hurt himself.

Rachel knew he was angry, but she had also been upset and had only him to blame. How dare he put on an act for the town and pretend to be so pious after what he'd done to her. Rachel thought she'd laugh if he crashed her door and ended up in the floor. After repeating his warning, Jesse pushed and the door opened. As he fell forward, Rachel stumbled toward him, hoping to break his fall.

At least I'll keep him from ripping his new suit.

As he fell into the room, Jesse staggered against Rachel and grabbed for the sofa. After gaining control, he stood up. Holding her, he smoothed her hair with his free hand and drew her to him with one arm, pressing her against his chest. He laughed at the shaken woman. "I tried to protect you and the living room but somebody has already destroyed it." He turned her head and forced her to meet his eyes. Rachel twisted from his embrace.

As Jesse studied the chaos before him, he knew something had happened before he arrived. His hand touched his brow. "Heavens, Rachel! What happened today?" He thought the house had surely been vandalized. Rachel stood quietly, as his eyes slowly surveyed the room. He noticed a small fire burning brightly in the limestone fireplace and large green wreaths tied with velvet bows at every window. This was home. Steedmore was a rambling dwelling, lacking warmth and feeling. Hearing Rachel's cough, he turned to see her blotched and tearstained face. She had definitely been upset over something and he was going to get to the root of it before the night was over. Had someone followed her home?

"Rachel, I just asked what happened. Was your house vandalized? Is that your problem? Have you been hurt?"

"N . . . Nothing happened here. And it's none of your business if it did."

Highly concerned, he growled, "Oh, yes, it is! So tell me about it. In fact, I've got nothing better to do, than listen to you." Jesse fluffed the throw pillow in a chair as if making his bed for the night. It was evident to him she had been lying on the sofa. He could almost make out the indentations of her body in the softness of the velvet. Dark splotches marked the red pillows and were proof she had been crying. Something that day had greatly upset her and Jesse hoped it had not been anything he'd said or done, even though she'd certainly been upset during the parade. His troubled eyes met hers.

"Did some man say something to you back there or did one of them try to take advantage of you? What about the man you romanced?"

"No!" Rachel put her hands to her ears, as if to shut out his words.

His voice grew louder as he placed his hands on her shoulders. "Then

Return to Leiper's Fork

what was done that upset you? I tried to get away but I couldn't. The Tennessean wanted to take pictures and interview me, and all the time I wanted to be with you. Rachel, we've got to talk."

"I don't think you have anything I want to hear and I certainly don't have anything to say to you, Jesse! I said nothing happened. What more do you want to know?" She pushed away from his grasp.

Jesse's eyes narrowed, as he spat out his words. "Why don't you let me in on your little secret? By the way you're looking and acting, I'd be blind not to know something has upset you. It looks like your purse and heels had an accident with an innocent Christmas tree and I want to know what caused it." Reaching down he picked up her black leather purse and placed the scattered contents in it. He zipped it and set it on the table, then reached for a red heel, which had landed on top of a wrapped gift. He found the other dangling precariously in the branches of the tree. A smiling angel with outspread wings was leaning to one side and as Jesse reached for it, a folded piece of paper fell from the bottom. He picked it up and laid it on a table then gently positioned the angel on top of the tree and turned to Rachel. "I suppose you have a broom around here somewhere?" He pointed to the broken glass ornaments near the tree. Not hearing a response, he searched the pantry and found the needed items.

Hurrying back, he noticed a small display on a table. A train was making its way around a village, which had a large lit Christmas tree. Rachel's eyes watched, as Jesse, drawn to the display held a broom in one hand and a dustpan in the other. She slowly walked to where he was standing. Jesse was a very handsome man. Perfect in every way. She liked the way his suit fit him and as she closed her eyes, she remembered his scent. His smoky gray eyes that could be stormy were now tender and his broad shoulders looked strong enough to carry the weight of the world. The very thought of being with him made her shiver. He pulled off his jacket and rolled the cuffs of his white shirt, then loosened his tie. He reached out a hand to touch her tear stained face, but Rachel pushed him away. "No, Jesse!"

"Angel, what made you cry?" Ignoring her silence, Jesse pointed to the sofa. "You don't usually sleep on your sofa in your Sunday clothing, do you?" He tried to smile but failed.

Rachel clenched her jaw and gave him a look of disgust but Jesse continued to prod. "Were you stood up by your date tonight? I mean, you're still nicely dressed. I thought you'd been waiting for the soldier you flirted with today."

Rachel's head jerked in surprise. Her eyes widened in disbelief. "What did you say, Jesse?"

"I asked, if you were stood up by your date. Remember the soldier you admired. Did you not tell him you couldn't wait? I believe you threw him a kiss. You refuse me and offer one to a total stranger. Did he find another woman he liked better than you? Maybe, one that was happy and fun to be with." An angry smile formed on Jesse's lips, as his face grew dark. The very thought of Rachel with another man filled him with jealousy.

"No, Jesse! I wasn't stood up by any man and that includes the soldier. I had my chances today but I don't date anymore. For your information, I haven't dated anyone since Carter but your calendar sure has been full. Men are the last thing I need, in case you're wondering." Large brown eyes glared at the man who was caught off guard by her words.

A questioning look crossed his face, as he placed his hands on his hips and stepped forward to grip her shoulders. Angry eyes pierced hers. "Is that the truth? You mean of all the chances you could have had to go out, you refused?"

"I guess that's right, Mr. Steed. I've had more important things on my mind. I had plenty of chances today and plenty others before you arrived. I'd be lying if I said I've not been lonely but I don't date, Jesse. I told you before, I am holding out for a man who will be a gift from God. Carter has been the only one since Randall. You know, I had a job to do at the museum and darn it, I did it and did it well." Rachel shook her head and threw up her hands. "It just doesn't matter anymore. I'm tired, and I need to go to bed." She held her head in her hands and exhaled. As Jesse watched, he noticed Rachel wipe her eyes. He knew he couldn't leave, regardless of how tired she was. He might not have this opportunity again.

"Do you have coffee in the kitchen?" He headed into the brightly colored kitchen without waiting for an answer and was amazed at how she had decorated her cabin. Red checked cushions covered the seats of tall ladder back chairs placed around a highly polished oak table. A red

Return to Leiper's Fork

poinsettia set in the center with red quilted place mats placed in front of each chair. Jesse breathed in the rich aroma of cinnamon and cloves which emanated from a large Christmas wreath on her back door. He slowly scooped coffee in the coffee maker and poured in fresh cold water. In a few moments, two, large brown reindeer mugs were full of coffee and set on the split log coffee table in the living room. After laying another log in the warm coals, he watched as Rachel forced wrinkles from her blouse. She slowly shook her head, as he handed her a cup of coffee. "Talk to me, princess. Please. I thought we were on the same page for a while. Weren't we?" His eyes pleaded with hers.

Coldly, she faced him and snapped her fingers. "What page was that, Jesse? I somehow can't remember. It's been a long time. Leave! I have better things to do."

"Does all of this have anything to do with me? Shake your head, 'Yes' or 'No.' You don't have to say a word."

Rachel jumped up, spilling her coffee in the process. "No, Jesse! No!"

"Well you're all wrong, Rachel. I think it does. There's a lot we need to unravel but first things first. I brought Lydia to Leiper's Fork. She wants to get married and I thought I was doing the right thing. In retrospect, I think I made a mistake." Jesse's words were cut short by Rachel, who was fighting to maintain control. Tears streamed down her face and he watched as red splotches covered her neck and face. Her body trembled as she placed her hands over her mouth. She was so angry she was afraid of what she might do. As she eyed a large glass vase, Jesse's face paled in the warm cabin. He watched silently as she tried to restrain her anger. He drew in a deep breath and raked his fingers through his thick hair.

Pointing a shaking finger, Rachel pushed her hair from her face, and tearfully stepped so near, he could feel her breath on his face. Thrusting her finger in his chest, she shouted, "Get out, Jesse! Get out of my life or I'll call the sheriff and have you arrested, tonight! If you don't think, I've got the guts to do it, watch me! Think how that would look in tomorrow's papers, Mr. Steed! You have caused me nothing but heartache. Go!"

She raced to her bedroom and the only other sounds he heard was a log shifting in the fireplace and the click of her bedroom door. Jesse tapped softly, hoping she would listen to him. "Please Rachel. I'm sorry if I've upset you. Don't make me leave, until we can get this straightened out. What did I say that hurt you?" He thought of pushing her door open but knew it would upset her more. Rachel covered her head with a pillow and sobbed.

Jesse continued tenderly but his words were wasted. "Lydia is not the woman I want to marry. She came to surprise, Tony. She has agreed to marry him and wanted to tell him in person. She's never flown before, so I told her she could come with me. I told him I was bringing her so he could plan a great weekend for her. Please, Rachel. Open the door. You're the only woman I've ever loved." He waited a few moments then stumbled blindly out her door.

What did I do? What did I say?

Return to Leiper's Fork

Chapter 20: Memories

Jesse left for Seattle and some folks said he'd never return to Leiper's Fork. Customers at The Country Store, said he looked like death warmed over, when he came in looking for something to eat.

"Haggard. That's the word I'd use for him. Real haggard, like. Never seen that man look so bad. Thought he was sick. Maybe that dedication was harder on him than we realized. Probably brought back too many memories about his parents."

"He bought a sandwich and a soda and walked out without taking his change."

Later, Steedmore, the historic mansion was emptied. Large trucks came and workers boxed and labeled every item in the house. For over two hundred years, the Steeds had lived on the property. Now it appeared a tornado had swept in and sucked every item into its funnel and carried it far away. Some said Jesse had taken it to an auction house in Nashville. Even the silk and velvet window treatments, which had hung for years, had been taken down and carried away. The old majestic house was deserted and the massive iron-gate that had guarded the curving driveway for a century was chained and locked. The folks in Leiper's Fork could not believe Jesse had done such a horrible thing.

"Deserted, that's what. Don't guess that little blonde Jesse brought with him liked Leiper's Fork after all."

"If Virginia Steed knew what her son did with all her stuff, she would roll over in her grave."

"Ain't that just like kids these days? You work all your life to get nice things and you die and your kids get rid of it before you're buried. Kids don't appreciate the fine things their parents had. They just up and sell it for nothing and go right out and pay a pretty penny for pressed wood and glue. Then they brag about their fine furniture from China."

"Wonder what Jesse did with all that silver, Virginia prized?"

As Rachel drove past the huge mansion, she gazed at the spacious yard, where generations of Steed children had rolled snowballs in winter and hunted colored eggs in the spring. Memories flooded her. She had visited Steedmore many times when she and Jesse dated. She had visited every room in the gigantic mansion and seen the fine antiques and European draperies. How often she and Jesse swam in the heated pool and feasted on chicken sandwiches afterward.

She remembered the day she and her mother brought food to the family after the death of Jesse's parents. That was the first time she had seen Jesse, since high school graduation. Grief had clouded his handsome features but he looked much the same as he always had. His shoulders were broader and he had grown taller but his eyes were still a beautiful steel gray. The cowlick in his dark hair was still prominent and his dimple in his chin was as endearing as always. His golden skin was tanned from the beautiful California sun. He'd stopped walking after noticing her on the drive. Rachel had seen his eyes glow momentarily then the fire had flickered and died. Without thinking, Jesse had pulled her close. It had only seemed natural at the time. After all, she was the woman he still loved. And then, the inevitable happened to spoil their moment. Mrs. Locke stepped out of the house and insisted they hurry home. What might have happened, if her mother had not surprised them? Rachel blushed to think that Jesse might have kissed her. Would she have changed her mind about marrying Randall? Could she have pulled away and would she have wanted to? At his parents' funeral, he had simply grasped her hand and murmured his thanks. His once sparkling gray eyes had been hollow and vacant and he seemed so far away. Later, she heard he had married Susanna Southhall and traveled to Europe.

The next time she saw Jesse was six years later. He had heard of Randall's death and flown in from San Francisco to offer his condolences. In Rachel's grief, she had chased him away but not before she saw concern in his gray eyes. How angry she'd been, after hearing Jesse was gobbling up hundreds of acres to build overpriced homes and possibly a shopping mall at Leiper's Fork. Adding to the acres he'd inherited from his parents, Jesse Steed was set to make millions of dollars. Leiper's Fork would never be the

Return to Leiper's Fork

same _ never a place of wild flowers, scenic hills, farms and gurgling creeks.

The night he appeared at the coffee shop was a night she'd never forget. She'd recognized his voice immediately but hoped he would not notice her. Then he had sauntered over to her table. The moment had seemed magical and she'd felt breathless, as she gazed into the face of a tired but very handsome man. He was impeccably dressed in a gray suit and when he smiled, a glow formed inside her. Jesse, the man she'd loved was now beside her and it was like old times. He had changed in many ways, yet he was the same Jesse _ handsome, easy to talk to, laughing, smiling, and serious. Did she miss him? He had seemed genuinely glad to see her and the camaraderie between them was as it had been when they dated. They'd shared their life and sipped coffee. He'd been so casual when the student suggested taking a picture of them. Jesse had smiled, lovingly kissed her hair and told her she could put the picture by their bed when he was away. She remembered how embarrassed she'd been when he'd insinuated, he was her husband. Later, he'd told her to think nothing of it. He was only pretending. He had played his part as usual, making her feel attractive once again and she'd felt like a million dollars. In the dark of night, he'd walked her to her car and stood watching, as she drove away. He'd tried to warn her about Carter and even insisted she leave with him when Carter had been angry. Hadn't Jesse always loved her? Hadn't she always loved him? The photo he had sent had been quietly tucked away.

Jesse! I was so blind. You did love me.

He had returned to Leiper's Fork several times and even though the project had been top secret, Jesse had made up for everything by dedicating the museum and the grounds to the town and Randall. She remembered the night of the dedication. How horrified she had felt when she looked in the mirror after he left. Jesse had not laughed or made fun of her swollen eyes or her wrinkled clothing. And her living room! She had not meant to kick the tree and sling her purse but it had happened. Through it all, Jesse's only concern had been for her. He had been extremely concerned about another man bothering her. Patiently, he had cleaned up the broken glass, picked up her purse and shoes and set the room in order. Jesse, a multi-millionaire had threatened to bust down her door, cleaned her living room, made coffee and tried to console her, but she had escaped to her bedroom, refusing to listen to him. The next morning, she had found the note Randall had placed inside the angel, the Christmas before he died. Jesse, not realizing it had been written by Randall, laid it on a table.

Precious Angel,
 When you read this, I'll be gone but I want you to know, I love you. It will be Christmas when you find this. I hope you're happy. Don't overlook the greatest gift of all _ love.
 Randall

She remembered Jesse, silently watching the Polar Express after he'd made coffee. The room had been dark, except for one lamp and a lighted table top display of a small train chugging around the base of a large Christmas tree. The tree, decorated with tiny twinkling lights and gold tinsel stood in the middle of a village and if one pulled the gold ticket, the train would whistle and a conductor would shout, "All aboard for the Polar Express!"

She remembered how Jesse's eyes had been glued to the Hallmark creation. "Is that the Polar Express, Rachel?"

"Y . . . Yes!"

He had spoken so tenderly. "I loved the book. I still have it at the house, somewhere." At that moment, he'd remembered a gift his parents had given him _ a large picture book, The Polar Express. He said he'd read it over and over again through the years. His tired eyes had glowed, as he stared at the train and watched it race around the tree. For a moment, he looked like a little boy at Christmas. It had been a bitter sweet moment for him as he'd smiled then turned away.

How difficult Christmas must be for him.

She'd broken the silence. "Randall bought this for me two years ago. When I saw it, I loved it and Randall had it wrapped and put under the tree. We watched that train for hours on Christmas morning. He said when I felt lonely, I should pull the gold ticket and all of my sadness would disappear."

Rachel remembered Jesse's question. "Did it?" In anticipating her answer, he'd leaned forward to watch the wave of emotion sweep over her beautiful face. Then he'd trailed his to her lips. Jesse had reached out to

Return to Leiper's Fork

her but she'd been jealous of Lydia, especially when he said he had brought her home to Leiper's Fork. She remembered escaping to her bedroom. She could not bear to hear him talk about marrying the beautiful, vivacious Lydia. That had been seven days ago and evidently he had left to get married. She'd heard gossip about Steedmore and how everything had been removed. She must forget him but it would be difficult.

When I know for sure I love him, it's too late.

The next day, Rachel heard the squeal of brakes and watched as a delivery truck pulled into her drive. One burly driver jumped out and knocked on her door, as the other lifted the overhead door of the truck.

"Miss Rachel Benton?" The man fingered an invoice then chewed on his cigar.

Rachel looked him in the eye. "The one and only. The only problem is I don't remember ordering anything. Are you sure you have something for me?"

The barrel-chested man, whose head appeared to rest on his shoulders, scratched his head. "Sure we do, darling. We were given explicit instructions to treat this thing like a baby and hang it over your fireplace mantle. If it's alright with you, we'll bring in the crate. Boss man said to tell you there is an envelope taped to the back of the frame and you must read it."

As the two men gently removed the object from its crate, Rachel gasped in surprise. "My painting!" In disbelief, she stepped back. "I can't believe this. It was sold months ago."

"Lady, we have instructions to hang it over the fireplace but first you need to remove that envelope on the back." The burly driver stood back and shifted his weight from one foot to the other. He watched as she gently, almost reverently removed the tape and lifted the envelope. She caught her breath when she recognized the writing and caught a faint whiff of Jesse's cologne.

Dear Rachel,
    By now you have received, your painting and are reading the note I attached. I'm

sure you're wondering what all of this is about. I could not allow just anyone to purchase that painting the day of the exhibit. I saw the attention it was receiving and I had to buy it before anyone else. You painted it in your grief and you named it correctly. The painting is about Leiper's Fork and your promise to protect our beautiful historic town. The skies have certainly loomed dark overhead, especially when you didn't understand what I was doing but as you can see in the painting, the golden sun has pierced the darkness. Leiper's Fork is blessed with sunshine. God will reveal the depth of all this to you one day, because He is a God who keeps his promises. When it happens, you will be free to love and live. Consider this painting an early Christmas gift and enjoy it for a life time. It comes with all my affection.

Jesse

PS I'm sure you'll remember the picture your student took in the coffee shop. For some strange reason, I thought you might like to have it. You are beautiful.

Rachel studied the smiling couple. Jesse had his arm around her shoulder and he looked as if he had won the lottery. She also was smiling. How happy she had felt that night. It seemed right to be with him. Tears stung her eyes, as she stood up.

I guess Lydia made him return it. He's a married man now. I didn't dream, Jesse was the one who purchased the painting. How can I ever thank him for saving it for me?

Rachel heard a cough. "Well, lady, we can stand here all day or get to doing what we've been paid to do. If there's one thing I hate to see, it's a woman crying. Are you going to be okay?" She nodded her head. The barrel chested man nervously positioned his weight on one foot then the other. Finally he twirled his cold cigar and shifted it to the other side of his mouth. He lifted his eyes to signal the other worker and nodded his head slowly. They had to get the painting on the fireplace in the next few minutes. Numerous boxes had to be delivered and quitting time was far from over.

Rachel looked at the burly man and could tell he was uncomfortable. "I understand. I'm not trying to hold you men up. I'm just a bit overwhelmed to get this back."

The logs in the fireplace crackled and popped. They too, seemed happy to have the painting where it belonged. Hours passed and the glowing embers slowly died. As Rachel sat on the velvet softness of her sofa, she thought of Jesse and all she owed him. She knew, she could never repay him but in the future she could send him some money. If she never received another gift in her life, the painting would make up for it.

Return to Leiper's Fork

That Sunday after church service, Rachel turned down numerous invitations to lunch. She wanted to be alone with her thoughts. In her cabin, she picked up, The Tennessean. Slowly, she read each page. It was better than going to bed early or sitting in front of a TV all evening. She knew she'd not be able to sleep regardless of what she did. In the society columns, a picture caught her eye. "Curator Takes Bride."

There before her was Tony, standing beside a beautiful woman wearing a strapless wedding gown. She clutched a large bouquet of calla lilies and roses. As Rachel read the article, she found the couple had married in Seattle and Jesse had been the best man.

"That rascal! He never told me he was in love, much less getting married. Let me see if I know the bride." Much to Rachel's astonishment, the bride was none other than the gorgeous, Lydia. As her eyes opened in surprise, she heard herself say, "I thought Lydia was marrying Jesse! How did this happen? Tony, you were in love with Lydia all the time we worked together, but you were so shy. You never told me and if you had, all of this would never have happened."

A bigger fool, than I, could never be found in the hills of Tennessee. All this time it's been Tony and Lydia instead of Jesse and Lydia. Now, I have driven Jesse away. He will never speak to me again.

Color flooded her face, as she wondered what Jesse, Tony and Lydia thought of her.

Chapter 21: The Promise

The cold wind blew and the weather forecast predicted snow for the Christmas holidays. Rachel threw another log on the fire and watched the embers blaze. Their crackling sound filled the cabin. She had cleaned house all afternoon and stood back admiring the cabin she loved so well. Fat candles, with the scent of vanilla glowed on the mantle, as Rachel breathed in the fresh Christmas scents. She noticed the homemade Christmas cookies, cooling on the counter and laughed at how she had made them. Some were shaped like stars, angels and reindeer, while some were plump Santa's, iced and ready to eat. Fresh hazelnut coffee was in the carafe and even the cabin creaked with joy, as it withstood the cold December wind.

The skies turned a darker shade of gray and Rachel with cup in hand, retreated to her living room and turned on her stereo. Soon, Christmas music filled the warm room as a light scattering of snowflakes fell from the skies. As she watched them drift slowly downward, she realized how much she loved her Tennessee cabin _ her little bit of Heaven on earth.

Rachel stared at the painting, the men had hung. How she had painted nearly four days was a mystery. Painting had been her outlet during her grief and when the work was completed, Rachel had collapsed in exhaustion. When she studied her work later, she stepped back in astonishment. There before her was Leiper's Fork. The sky was indeed overcast, even somber, but through the gloomy gray ash of the heavens, sunshine pierced through and streamed on the clapboard church below. She gasped after remembering Randall's words.

When you see Heaven smiling, know I'm happy. Remember, when you see the sunshine you can be happy about your life. You'll know joy once again after I'm gone . . . remember the sunshine.

"Randall! I know you are happy and you want me to be happy. Were you saying more than you realized at the time? I have grieved for you and kept you in my heart. I thought I loved Carter but it was only a silly infatuation. I will always keep you in my heart even though I love Jesse. Today, I must move forward with my life. I know you are happy. Thank

Return to Leiper's Fork

you for showing me the sunshine, my precious darling."

Wrapping a red wool scarf around her neck, Rachel hurried out to her car. She didn't have time to change clothes now. Her eyes sparkled and in the frosty air she could see her breath rise up in front of her. Winter's brush had painted her cheeks a rosy red and she'd never felt more alive. Putting her car in four wheel drive, she carefully made her way down the lane and onto Old Hillsboro Road. Already, the flakes were building and covering the houses and businesses. The Christmas lights beamed along Old Hillsboro and made different colors on the snow that was slowly drifting in the road. She wondered if she should not turn back but knew she wasn't going too far. The smell of fried chicken filled the air and she noticed the ottoman from Serenite Maison's was absent from the widow. "I know I should have bought it. Next time, Rachel, don't wait."

After a few moments, she veered into the small cemetery and briskly walked to the grave site she had visited numerous times in the last year and a half. Her voice cheerful rang out, "Randall, I'm here to wish you, Merry Christmas. I'm sure you're up there rejoicing but I wanted to tell you something. If Jesse will forgive me and ask me to marry him, I will accept. Somehow, I've always loved him, but I loved you too, Randall. Jesse has taken good care of me since you left and he will make a wonderful husband and father. I only hope I have not waited too long." Rachel kissed her hand and touched the pink granite stone, which had a thin white icing of snow. In minutes, her car was turned toward Steedmore.

To her amazement, both gates stood open, as if expecting her. Rachel could not believe her luck. "Since you are waiting for me, I will drive on in and pretend I own this place." She laughed. For the first time in a year and a half a burden lifted from her shoulders. Rachel felt light, free and happy. As she ascended the hill, the sprawling house covered in white loomed before her.

What a picturesque postcard! Steedmore and all of its trees and greenery, covered in white snow at Christmas. One day I'd like to capture it on canvass.

After noticing a small car parked at the back, Rachel was sure a realtor was visiting the home. She slowly opened her car door, to receive a small plop of snow on her shoulder. Brushing it off, she laughed to herself and called out in the snowy silence, "I'm home, honey."

From the edge of the wood, came a man's response. "I'm glad you're home. What's for supper? I'm tired after a long day's work." Jesse stood near the trees wearing faded jeans, and a blue jacket. A red wool scarf was hanging loosely around his neck and delicate snowflakes lay on top his dark hair. His face was red from the cold but he was smiling and his sparkling gray eyes flashed a warm welcome.

Rachel's smile froze, as she spun around to the man standing by a large spruce. "Jesse! What are you doing here?"

He shook the snow from his hair and stamped his boots, while approaching her. With a gloved hand, he pointed. "Rachel, you're always asking the wrong question. I need to ask you, what you're doing here." A wry smile played on Jesse's lips, as his questioning eyes searched hers. He drew closer and as he did, Rachel's face turned crimson _ the color of her woolen scarf. She'd made a fool of herself and Jesse had the upper hand. She should never have come but she would leave quickly. She wondered what had possessed her to enter those iron gates.

She stammered at Jesse's continued stare, wondering if she should make a dash for her car. "Well, uh, I'm not sure why I came up the drive. I just wanted to see Steedmore one last time and the gate was open. I thought if I could see it up close, I would paint it one day. But you're here. I heard you had s . . . sold everything and the house is empty. Why did you return?

Jesse stroked his jaw, as he studied her quivering lips. "Well you're half right, Rachel. The house is empty. I also wanted to have one last look before I left for good. I lived here for almost twenty years and it is an old home. Outdated by a hundred and fifty years but with a little work and a fantastic decorator, it could be a beauty again. I know the rumors going around but I didn't sell the furniture. I had it packed and placed in storage. You see, my wife might want some of those antiques. I'd prefer she select the pieces she'd like. If she wanted to live here, I'd be happy but if not, I'm comfortable wherever I lay my head. I just want her to be happy."

Rachel's heart fell. Jesse was talking about his wife. Had he found someone else to love and marry? Had there been someone waiting behind the scenes for Jesse all along? Possibly, someone in Seattle? When she sent

Return to Leiper's Fork

him away, he'd given up and married. Rachel knew in her heart, she had waited too long. Jesse was making other plans for his life and rightly so.

Too late, Rachel. A good man won't wait forever. Too late! Too late!

Rachel found it hard to look in his eyes but from somewhere, she gathered a little strength. She straightened her shoulders and smiled. "Jesse, your wife is a very blessed woman. She couldn't have found a more thoughtful and wonderful man. Th . . . Thank you for the painting. I want to pay you back someday because you paid a lot of money for it. Even I know it wasn't worth what you paid but you kept me from losing my mind and my house. I don't know if you knew it or not but it was so embarrassing when everyone was discussing my financial situation. I did everything I could but I couldn't borrow from Mom or Dad. When you asked me to paint the murals it was a godsend. I paid off my mortgage ." Rachel watched the man standing before her. Dressed in faded jeans he was a handsome sight to see. Apparently, he had not shaved for several days, but she thought he was more appealing. As he studied her face, she grew self-conscious.

"What?" Had she smeared her lipstick, or had her mascara failed her again? Jesse touched her pink lips, causing her to tremble.

"Are you cold?" Quietly, he reached out to draw her close and began rubbing her cold arms briskly. "By the way, you don't owe me anything. I was going to donate the painting to the museum but as I prayed that morning, I knew where that painting belonged. It had to hang over your fireplace. It's all about God's promise to you." As gray eyes searched brown ones, a hint of a smile played on his lips. He cupped her face in his hands and as the wind ruffled her golden brown hair, he reached out to touch its silky strands. He watched as Rachel nervously bit her lower lip and the familiar flush crept up her face.

"Jesse, you can't do this when you're married."

His eyes registered surprise but he ignored her comment. "Do you want to tell me why you came?" Jesse smiled mysteriously but Rachel looked away. How could she tell him what was in her heart and what she told Randall at the cemetery? It was too late. The damage was already done and

Jesse belonged to a woman he'd vowed to honor and love forever. Hadn't her own father told her Jesse wouldn't wait forever?

"Tonight, I was looking at the p . . . painting. I saw the gray clouds covering Leiper's Fork and I thought how difficult the last year and a half had been. I thought of Randall's words, when he told me to watch for the sunshine because I would know he was happy and he wanted me to be happy. Jesse, I have been so miserable for such a long time." Rachel's eyes brimmed with tears but she held up her hand to hold him back, as he stepped forward. "I have acted like such a fool. I thought you were in love with Lydia and then I read where she and Tony had married. How could I have been so confused and caused so much turmoil? Now, you're married."

Moving closer, Jesse touched her face then placed his hands on her warm neck. "Rachel, I know you loved Randall. Probably always will in many ways, but I couldn't compete with a dead man. I tried but failed. When you fell in love with Carter, it nearly killed me but thank goodness you saw him for what he was. I never told you but it was Lil who did his paintings for him the last year and a half. He knew several were required each year to stay in good standing with his college and medically he was unable to do it. I'm not an artist but I knew this last one was not his work. He is a very sick man, Rachel. I pray he gets the help he needs and I thank God every day, He protected you." He stepped back and stroked his jaw.

"When I saw the Polar Express, it reminded me of my life. Round and round and round again. I was leaving for good and making my home in Seattle but I needed to come one last time. I finally got that pilot's license I've been working on for the last year. Now, I won't have to wait in an airport for hours. I'm here for the day but I needed to see the old home place one more time. I don't know how long I will be in Seattle but probably until we get more of that gas flowing and those prices down. You see, Dad and my uncles formed a company, years ago. They knew there was oil in Canada. Rachel, it has finally happened and I've been busy seeing that the oil is pumped into freighters and sent on down to Houston, to the refinery. I was, pumping gas, as I told you."

Rachel blanched. "Jesse. What a fool I have been thinking you were working in a gas station. I'm sorry for all the embarrassment I have cost you. Like a fool, I took everything you offered and threw it away. I've made your life miserable. If I had another chance, I would give up everything, even Leiper's Fork, for you but it's too late." A flicker of

Return to Leiper's Fork

surprise crossed Jesse's face. Was this the same Rachel who swore she would never leave? "I hope you're happy because you deserve all of the happiness in the world. Goodbye, Jesse." Rachel reached up to kiss the stunned man on the cheek then turned toward her car.

"Rachel." Gently, Jesse pulled her to him. "Yes, I spoke of my wife. She is blessed because I love her more than life itself. I want to spend the rest of my life with her. I want her to be truly devoted to me because I'd give up everything I owned for her. That's how I feel about the woman I love."

Rachel nodded as a lump filled her throat. "I wish you and your wife all the joy in the world, Jesse." She pulled away and turned toward her car.

Exhaling, he ran his hand through his hair. "Honey, you don't understand. This morning at the hotel, God woke me and told me to come to Steedmore. As I was walking from the wood, I saw your car come up the drive and God spoke clearly. 'Your bride is approaching. Tell her you love her and take her in your arms. Her time of grieving is over and so is your wait for your bride. She is yours, now.' He smiled and caressed her arms.

Rachel searched his gray eyes. "W . . . What? Are you talking about me? Are you telling me you're not married?"

"Well, not yet. You see, honey, it's like Isaac and Rebecca. He was in the fields watching for his bride when she arrived riding on a camel, accompanied by his father's servant. She knew God had a plan and a husband who would love her. You came to me when I was standing in the field and I know you love me. Honey, I have always loved you. Will you marry me? I want the world to know that you belong to me. Will you make me the happiest man in the world? I have waited all these years for you." Jesse embraced her and prayed to hear the right words.

"Jesse! How can I say, 'No?' Yes, I will marry you but I need a wedding gown." She smiled. "I think I can find one in Nashville."

At that moment, a shaft of golden sunlight pierced through the blanket of dark gray that flooded Leiper's Fork. As they stood in the sunshine, covered in snowflakes, two people were thrilled with the decision they had made. Rachel drew Jesse's face, to hers. "Randall told me when I see the sunshine, I'd be happy and I am. I'm marrying the man, I love."

After kissing every snowflake from her face, Jesse responded, "And I'm marrying the woman I've always loved. Honey, can I come to your house in a bit? I have a Christmas gift for you and I want you to open it. You see, I ordered it the day of the Christmas Parade and I didn't know what to do, if you wouldn't marry me."

Jesse held her hand, as they walked to her car. "I need to check the house one last time, before I come over. Only fix coffee. We can eat later."

That night, Jesse scooped up his future bride, as she met him at the door. Together, they planned a simple wedding at the white clapboard church in the middle of town. Jesse asked if they could have cupcakes instead of the traditional wedding cake. "German Chocolate is my favorite."

Rachel assured him that would be special and they could drink tea from fruit jars and have barbeque and all the sides. "We'll have our wedding just the way we want it. Maybe, have burlap placemats, too." Rachel laughed at the thought of having a plain and simple down home wedding when Jesse could afford the most elaborate wedding, Tennessee had ever witnessed.

"Rachel, I need to be in Seattle for two weeks after our honey moon but I want to make our home in Leiper's Fork. We can build on to the cabin, have the cabin moved to Steedmore or sell the cabin and live at Steedmore. You decide. There needs to be some updating at the old house and you can decide how you want to decorate. I have Mom's furniture and you can select what pieces you want. If you don't want any of it, we'll sell it. I don't care where we live and in which house, as long as I live with you. When I travel, you can join me until our children are born. I just want us to be together." Then he smiled and kissed her. "When I'm away, you can place that photo of us on your nightstand and dream of me. I hope you still have it." They laughed and Jesse pulled her close. "I made a copy and it is on my nightstand in Seattle. Every night, I kissed my angel before I went to bed and every morning I kissed her when I woke up. She was never far from me but I couldn't tell her about it."

That night, as Rachel filled their mugs and chose a few more Christmas cookies from the platter, she saw Jesse holding a gold foil gift as she entered the room. "Open it, honey. I picked it out for you at, Serenite Maison's."

Return to Leiper's Fork

Jesse's eyes were full of excitement.

As she feasted on the beautiful charm bracelet nestled in blue silk, Rachel's eyes were damp with tears. "Jesse! What a precious gift." She lifted the gold bracelet which resembled tiny branches entwined with each other. Small gold charms dangled from it.

Jesse pointed to the charms. "Rachel, I selected several of these because I didn't want you to miss Leiper's Fork when we are away on business." Each gold charm had been delicately inscribed, noting special events in their lives and the names of Leiper's Fork most prominent businesses. He showed her each charm but saved one until last. Rachel kissed him as he held it between his fingers. "Honey, remember the restaurant in Houston where the future groom had to prove the diamond was real? Remember, he etched the initials on the window pane of the school? I wanted our initials on your charm bracelet. I hope you will wear your bracelet and know how very much I love you and Leiper's Fork." He hesitated and pulled a small ring box from his pocket. "I want to give you a very special diamond that belonged to Mother. It's a square cut stone , so I hope you like it."

No woman could have been happier than Rachel Benton, when Jesse Steed placed the sparkling diamond on her finger. "Sealed with love, my precious. Sealed with all the love in my heart." Tears filled his eyes, as he held the woman he had waited so long to call his own.

Rachel choked back her own tears. "If you only knew how much I love you. I thank God. He saved you for me and answered my prayer. You have made me the happiest woman in Leiper's Fork. I hope I can make you a very happy man."

He cupped her chin and kissed her. "Honey, I am a happy man but I'm also the hungriest. Let's go down to Puckett's for supper. I think a band is playing there tonight."

As soft music played, Jesse cocked his ear and took another sip of iced tea. He smiled and pulled her close. "Honey, I think they are playing our song. Listen." Jesse hummed with the music.

"Jesse, he may be singing, Rocky Top Tennessee, is home sweet home but Leiper's Fork is home sweet home, to us. Regardless of where we go, it will always be our home." She shook the gold charm bracelet on her wrist and reached over to give Jesse a kiss on his lips.

"Honey, you couldn't be more right." Jesse's eyes twinkled. "I've been all over the world but I had to come home to Leiper's Fork, to marry the woman, I've always loved."

With a crowded restaurant, the news of their wedding spread quickly and the band insisted on playing a special song for the engaged couple. Jesse requested, *I Hope You Dance*. Taking Rachel's hand, Jesse led her to the dance floor and pulled her close. "Honey, I remember the night of the reunion. I flew all the way from Seattle, hoping I could hold you for one dance but you refused. It was one of the saddest days of my life. I beat myself up for days."

"Jesse, you can dance with me the rest of my life. I can't think of a better place to be, than in the arms, of the man I love."

By midnight, many in Leiper's Fork had heard of the engagement and Rob, the owner of Puckett's insisted he was picking up the tab for their meal. One of the richest men in the United States was having dinner in his restaurant tonight and he wasn't going to forget it. "Listen son. You keep that Canadian oil coming on down the pipe and Shanel and I will give you free burgers or fried chicken for the rest of your life. We're all counting on you. Besides, this is the place to come if you want your blood pressure lowered." He chuckled and ran his hand over his beard, then adjusted his cap. "You know, you two are welcome to dance here anytime but Jesse, I'd recommend a few more lessons for you."

Jesse slapped him on the back and ushered his fiancé out the door. Never had there been a greater evening and Jesse knew there were plenty more to come. Soon Rachel would be his bride.

Return to Leiper's Fork

Chapter 21: The Dance

A few days later, Rachel Benton became the bride of Jesse Steed, descendent of Colonel Jesse Steed, one of Leiper's Fork earliest settlers.

As Rachel nervously walked down the church aisle on the arm of her father, everyone in Leiper's Fork was watching. The bride had chosen a couture gown with tiny strands of blue woven into it. She'd had a silk tag stitched inside that read, **Mrs. Jesse Steed/2012**. The bride wore white slippers which matched her gown and each had a blue bow at the heel. Her beautiful, golden brown hair was swept away from her face and her only jewelry was the matching pearl earrings and necklace which Jesse's mother and grandmother had worn on their wedding day. At the last minute, Mrs. Locke pressed a pale blue handkerchief in Rachel's hand.

Something old, something new, something borrowed, something blue.

Jesse watched from the front of the church, as he stood near the pastor and Tony Hunter. His eyes misted when he saw Rachel reach the door. He had waited years for this moment and it was finally happening. His heart pounded as he saw her search for him at the front. As he turned to Tony and wiped his eyes, Tony gripped his hand and whispered, "You lucky devil. You owe me. I told everybody who even looked at her, if they dared ask her out, I'd let the air out of their tires and have them fired. I expect a steak dinner after you get back from the honeymoon." Jesse nodded.

Now, his bride, the woman of his dreams was slowly coming toward him. Jesse smiled, remembering he was wearing the blue shirt she had asked him to wear. She in turn was wearing the silk gown she hoped, he'd love. As she and her father reached the center of the aisle, Rachel hesitated and turned toward Bill who had her arm softly nestled in his. Her face flushed, as he reached over to adjust her veil. She moistened her lips, all the while searching her father's eyes. Was she doing the right thing? Had she waited long enough after Randall's death? Did she really love Jesse? Bill

Locke had the answers to the myriad of questions he read in her eyes. Rachel glanced at the beautiful Betsy dressed in a rose silk. Betsy gave her the thumbs up signal and pointed to Jesse who was wiping his brow.

Bill Locke patted his daughter's arm and whispered, "Yes, daughter. He's the man, God saved for you. Listen to your heart. You've always loved him and Jesse has always loved you. Now, you've got a lifetime together. Cherish each moment and never question his love."

As Rachel and her father reached the front of the church, Rachel grasped Jesse's hand. He pulled her close. "Princess, I thought you'd never get here. If you had gone in the opposite direction, I would have run after you. I kept praying and praying you'd come to me and you did."

Rachel smiled radiantly as Jesse, noticing her damp lashes tenderly wiped her eyes with his blue handkerchief.

The pastor smiled and spoke to the wedding guests. "Folks, they're not married yet, but Jesse is already drying the tears of this beautiful woman. I was told that Jesse promised Rachel years ago, if she would marry him, he'd give her Leiper's Fork and lay it at her feet." He smiled at the blushing couple and looked at the guests who wondered what the pastor meant.

With a twinkle in his blue eyes, he turned to the man before him.
"When we make a promise to the woman we love, we keep it, don't we, Jesse?" The handsome groom nodded, wondering what Rachel was thinking.

Rachel's heart pounded as she whispered, "Jesse, it's not possible. I never expected you to . . . carry out what you said years ago." She glanced nervously around. Everyone was smiling, except the bride.

Jesse chuckled and pointed to the floor. As Rachel followed his eyes, she discovered a large map of Leiper's Fork beneath her feet. Her laugh was angelic. Jesse wrapped his arms around her and gave her a kiss.
"Remember, I always keep my promises."

Rachel whispered, "I'm glad you did. You've made me your bride and thrown in Leiper's Fork to boot."

During the wedding ceremony, the pastor whispered to Bill Locke,

Return to Leiper's Fork

who joined Jesse and Rachel. Nervously, Bill winked at Jesse and handed him a faded velvet bag. Rachel looked at her father, then back at Jesse. She had seen this bag before. Jesse took Rachel's hand in his. "My precious, my grandfather and father presented this bag of coins to their bride on their wedding day. It represented their commitment to marriage and their love to their bride. Today, I offer this same gift to you, as a symbol of my commitment and eternal love."

Later, the guests threw birdseed, as the happy couple emerged from the church and rode in a carriage down Old Hillsboro Road. Everyone in Leiper's Fork had been invited to the large wedding reception at the museum. A large silver tray held a figure of a bride and groom carved from one piece of wood, compliments of Bill Locke and numerous German Chocolate wedding cupcakes surrounded it. The tray set on top of an oak stump which had been beautifully preserved. The tree where two lovers carved their initials years before had been fashioned into a table for their cabin. Jesse had asked for the stump, hoping one day he could present it as a wedding gift to Rachel and Bill Locke had certainly worked his magic. He'd been only too happy to carry out his future son–in–law's wishes. When Jesse brought the stump to Rachel's attention, never had a bride been as stunned as Rachel. Tenderly, she traced their initials still evident after ten years.

After some time, Tony and Lydia delivered a long blue car to the front of the museum and made an announcement that the bride and groom were leaving for their honeymoon. After Jesse helped his bride into the Dresden Blue, Cadillac de Ville and took the wheel, he kissed her. "My dream has come true. At last you are mine, Mrs. Steed. I'm so happy you are with me in my favorite car. This is better than any prom or parade could ever be."

Some miles away, Jesse's company plane was awaiting the couple. Rachel's dream of a honeymoon in Charleston, South Carolina was finally coming true and she would be leaving with her pilot husband. After a few days in Charleston, they would fly to Seattle, so Jesse could oversee the transfer of oil from the Canadian pipeline. Later, after a huge renovation to their cabin, they would move into their beloved cabin. As for historic Steedmore, it was offered to the town as the new Leiper's Fork Country Club. A twenty-six room mansion with tennis courts and a swimming pool would make a perfect place for the community to host many gatherings.

The next evening, a young photographer pointed the camera at the happy couple as they stood near the Avenue of Oaks, on Boone Hall Plantation. As he held the camera, he asked a question. "Why did you two pick Charleston for your honeymoon?"

Rachel blushed as her husband answered without missing a beat. "She told me in high school if I married her, I'd have to take her to Charleston to see the Avenue of Oaks. Even though it has taken us a while to get here, I kept my promise. Nothing is too good for my Leiper's Fork bride. What do you think, Mrs. Steed?" Jesse turned to his bride of two days.

"If my husband makes a promise, he keeps it. Right, Mr. Steed?"

"I try, honey."

The young photographer responded with a grin. "I'm getting married soon. Would Leiper's Fork be a great place for a honeymoon?"

Jesse looked seriously at the photographer. His gray eyes sparkled. "I can only warn you of one thing. If you visit Leiper's Fork, you may never want to leave. Some of us call it, 'A Little Bit of Heaven.' With those words, he turned to Rachel and led his bride down the path beneath the ninety, moss covered oak trees. As the silver-green moss swayed in the soft southern breeze and the rays of sunlight filtered through the draping moss, Jesse pulled her close and held her hand to the last rays of the setting sun.

"That's a real stone, Mrs. Steed. I know how to prove it, if you'd like." He smiled and pointed to the sparkling panes of glass in the stately windows of the large, two story plantation house. The square cut diamond flashed brilliantly, as Rachel smiled into her husband's smoldering eyes.

"Jesse, you don't have to prove anything to me. Your word is more precious than the coins you gave me at our wedding." She pressed her head against his chest and heard the rumble of his laughter.

"Honey, I'm glad you decided to dance with me and not sit it out." He nuzzled her cheek and led her farther down the three-quarter mile path, beneath the majestic, live oak trees, crowned with swaying moss and lined with brilliant azaleas.

"Jesse, if I had not married you, I would have missed the dance of a

Return to Leiper's Fork

lifetime. I promise to love you forever and ever." Suddenly, the wind swirled Rachel's long white skirt and Jesse pulled her close. After whispering in her ear, they began to dance slowly beneath the oaks. Oaks planted forty-seven years before Colonel Jesse Steed settled in a tiny town known today as, Leiper's Fork.

Penny Garrison

Leiper's Fork, Tennessee
or

"A Little Bit of Heaven"

Leiper's Fork is a little bit different
We're laid back, a bit you see,
We sit on our porch in the evening
Pick guitars and drink sweet tea.
It's a place where friends and neighbors
Enjoy each other's company,
We're just a great, big happy family
In Leiper's Fork, Tennessee.
Instead of watching television
There's a whole lot more to see,
We've got raccoons, deer and wild turkey
Sunsets more beautiful than you can believe.
We still go to church on Sunday
We still pray down on our knees,
We love God, family and country
That's important and what we believe
The fiddler keeps on a fiddling
The tunes are dear as they can be,
And banjo players keep a strumming
'The Fork,' is where we love to be.
Mommas are a 'holding their babies
Getting ready for the jamboree,
Folks are kicking up their heels and dancing
In Leiper's Fork, Tennessee.
Our kids play in hills and hollers
Chase raccoons and shimmy up trees,
Swim in creeks and catch ole crawdads,
They're as happy as a kid can be.
And the flag of our dear country
Flies high for all to see,
And we sing our national anthem
We're Americans, and glad we're free.
Patriotism runs deep in our town

Return to Leiper's Fork

We love our soldiers, where 'ere they be,
You see, they protect us while we're sleeping
We feel safe in Tennessee.
So come on down and see us
Sit in our rockers, and drink an iced tea
Until we meet, we'll say, 'God bless you!'
Your friends, in Leiper's Fork, Tennessee.

Penny Garrison©

Other books by the author are:

1. *In the Shadow of the Columns*- an 1898 love story between an attorney and a destitute woman which takes place near Academic Hall, in Columbia, MO.

2. *A Louisiana Inheritance*- an 1840's house is inherited in Louisiana, MO, but what treasure, left by a great, great, aunt will be found in the basement? What secret will an engineer have that will keep him from falling in love with the woman he cannot forget ? What will she do when she finds out his secret?

3. *The Golden Thread*- A former slave during the Great Depression teaches two broken hearts how to trust and love. On Christmas Day, will both find happiness or will one leave with a broken heart?

4. *A Promise Kept*- (sequel to, The Golden Thread) When a husband leaves for WWII, what happens when he is declared dead but returns to find his wife engaged? How can he win her love the second time? Which of the two men will be waiting at the end of the runway when Shelby is forced to model a wedding dress fashioned from a silk parachute?

For more information about the books, go to *wwwww.pennygarrisonbooks.com*

Return to Leiper's Fork

Return to Leiper's Fork

Return to Leiper's Fork